Cold Hands

JOHN NIVEN

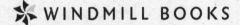 WINDMILL BOOKS

Published by Windmill Books 2014

8 10 9 7

Copyright © John Niven 2012

John Niven has asserted his right under the Copyright, Designs and
Patents Act, 1988, to be identified as the author of this work.

First published in Great Britain in 2012 by William Heinemann

First published in paperback in 2013 by Vintage

Windmill Books
The Random House Group Limited
20 Vauxhall Bridge Road, London SW1V 2SA

Addresses for companies within The Random House Group Limited can be found at:
www.randomhouse.co.uk/offices.htm

The Random House Group Limited Reg. No. 954009

www.randomhouse.co.uk

A CIP catalogue record for this book
is available from the British Library

ISBN 9780099592143

Typeset by Palimpsest Book Production Limited,
Falkirk, Stirlingshire

Printed and bound in Great Britain by Clays Ltd, Elcograf S.p.A.

MIX
Paper from
responsible sources
FSC® C018179
FSC
www.fsc.org

Penguin Random House is committed to a sustainable
future for our business, our readers and our planet.
This book is made from Forest Stewardship
Council® certified paper.

For my sister, Linda
A real girl

Had I thy brethren here, their lives and thine were not revenge sufficient for me. No, if I digged up thy forefathers' graves, and hung their rotten coffins up in chains, it could not slake mine ire, nor ease my heart.

Henry the Sixth, Part Three

Prologue

Coldwater, Florida; Present Day

IT'S WARM here, in Coldwater. I've lived in four different countries, if you count Scotland and England as separate countries – which most of us Scots would – but this is the first warm one. They say it's good for what's left of my leg.

Florida is a strip mall: stretches of highway lined with parking lots, the lots surrounded by eateries offering $3.99 breakfasts and Early Bird Specials, by drugstores bigger than the biggest supermarkets where I grew up: entire aisles of toothbrushes, walls of shampoo, the uncountable brands of mouthwash. Every hundred yards, it seems, there's the Colonel's face smiling down at you, or the blood-red, head-of-a-spot-yellow of another McDonald's. It's not the kind of place I thought I'd ever live but then, when I arrived here, just over a year ago, I didn't really care where I ended up.

With the two-year anniversary coming up Dr Tan thought it might help if I could stand to write it all down. I don't have to show it to anyone. Just put it all down on paper.

She thought it might help me to identify 'specific areas' I wanted to work on in our sessions. 'After all,' she said, 'you used to be a writer, didn't you?' Well, I managed a laugh at that.

I'm writing this at the desk in the little ground-floor bedroom I've made my office. It's really just a place where I come to read. The house is what they call 'colonial': lots of white oak, cool, light and airy. From my window I can see the jungly garden and the small egg-shaped pool. I can smell the azaleas, the beach. Cora, the housekeeper, comes every day. She's cheerful, black, small and wiry. She straightens the place up and fixes supper.

I'm writing longhand – my left hand still hurts too much for typing on the laptop; the deep, savage scar on my palm, going red when I make a fist, gradually whitening as I unclench it. I am forty-three years old, but I feel, and look, older, like I really have lived two lives concurrently. In strands and streaks, grey is threading through my hair at the temples. The pouches beneath my eyes are now unrelieved by sleep. Taxi drivers will say, 'You look tired, friend,' and it doesn't feel unusually rude. Finally, in the last two years, unable to exercise properly any more, flab has begun to pool and gather at my sides, at my waist. Lying in the bath the other day, straining forward to reach the taps, I found myself out of breath.

She said I didn't have to show it to anyone, but it has to be written *for* someone. All writing is aimed at someone. So who is this for? Who is its ideal reader? Walt? Sammy? Maybe Craig Docherty? Strangely, I think it's for *her*. For Gill. The account she was due. And where to begin? Where's the jumping-off point? The 'inciting incident'? (Ah, how fondly I remember those screenwriting manuals – Raymond G. Frensham, Syd Field, Denny Flinn – and their inscriptions: *'Happy birthday, Donnie, love S XXX (Just do it!)'* Relics of a happier time.) I should really start in Scotland, all those years ago, but I can't face going there right away. Better to start with the events that led up to that night. Which I think means starting with the dog.

We'll start with the dog.

1

Saskatchewan, Canada; Two Years Earlier
'DADDY, I can't find Herby.'

Slipping my cellphone into my pocket I turned around on the deck that ran the front length of the house, coffee mug in hand, steam rising into the November air, and looked down at Walt. He had a hand raised to shield his eyes from the morning sun reflecting crazy-brilliant off the snow. He was wearing his beige parka with fur trim and a blue Ralph Lauren scarf with a little teddy bear on it. His mittens dangled on strings from his sleeves, hung men, ghost hands echoing the real ones. Walt's thick fringe fell into his eyes, tea-coloured, an amalgam of his mother's muddy blonde and mine: black as burnt toast. My son would soon be nine and, thankfully, so far, it looked like he was inheriting his mother's hair, fine and silky, flopping naturally into a graceful parting. Not mine, this dry, wiry Scottish hair.

'He'll be around somewhere, Walt,' I said, stepping towards him, the snow styrofoam-squeaking beneath my boots. 'He's probably with one of the neighbours.'

Part of this was an outright lie – I had just rung both the Franklins and Irene Kramer that morning. Herby, our caramel Labrador was definitely not with either of them – and the rest of it was said with an assurance I did not feel. While it was true that Herby had run off several times before ('Saskatchewan is so flat,' the old joke goes, 'you can watch your dog run away from home for a week') and it was possible that the dog was somewhere on our five-acre property, he had never made off in winter before. It wasn't true Canadian winter yet – the temperature was still hovering above zero – but much worse was forecast for the weeks to come. We'd soon be into minus five and minus six and then the blizzards when the real winter began: fifteen, twenty below. Hoth.

'That's what Mommy said,' Walt began. I could see Sammy through the glass behind him, crossing the huge kitchen, heading for the sink, one of the sinks, to rinse a coffee cup. (Sammy is fastidious.) 'But what if –'

'Well, Mommy's probably right, huh? She usually is. Come on, let's go back in. It's cold and you're gonna be late for school.' I took a last look around the surrounding fields, hoping against hope to see the bronzed outline coming hopping towards us, tongue lolling. Nothing – just miles of snow.

The view from our deck was the reason Sammy wanted to build the house here; we're up on a ridge, looking down the valley with Lake Ire in the distance, fringed with pine trees, burning silver. The Franklin property is a mile and a half to our right; Irene's place, the old Bennett farmhouse, our closest neighbour, a half-mile to our left.

But nothing, no dog. (*Thinking back now my memory keeps trying to add something; black shapes wheeling in the sky, crows circling a spot down at the end of our field, towards Tamora Road, the main route in to town. But I cannot be sure that I saw this at the time.*)

I shepherded Walt through the sliding glass door – a door in an entire wall of glass that runs the length of the kitchen – and back into the warmth and scent of breakfast; toast, coffee and oatmeal, a bowl of which Sammy was finishing while she watched the small flatscreen TV that hung above the central island in the middle of the room. She was perched on the edge of the scrubbed oak table, her legs crossed at the ankles. Sammy was three years older than me, but looked several younger. (Lousy Scottish genes, I often thought, while being aware of the therapy cliché that when we blame our genes we're really blaming ourselves.) She wasn't conventionally beautiful and could quickly list you what she felt her defects were. Her teeth were too prominent, almost buckish, a trait she would hide touchingly by covering her mouth with her hand on the occasions when she laughed spontaneously and unreservedly. There was the faint tracery of acne scars in the hollows of her cheeks and the knotted furrow that appeared in the middle of her forehead when she was concentrating, or irritated. Sammy was tall, nearly six feet, a couple of inches taller than me, and, she felt, gangly. Self-conscious of this as a teen, she'd developed a slouching, stooped posture to try and disguise it, something she could still slip into now and then. She'd been a natural at sports, however – netball and lacrosse for her school – and still had something of the jock about her. She could beat me at a stroll on the tennis court: on vacation, at the club outside Alarbus, or at her parents' place, with her graceful positioning, that slight pause before she whipped the racket through, brushing up the ball, imparting topspin, sending me skittering back on my heels.

COLD HANDS

That morning, in the kitchen, her lips shone from the honey that glossed her oatmeal and her hair was scraped back into a taut ponytail. She was wearing a dark grey wool suit over a black V-neck sweater: a look from the smarter end of her business wardrobe. (I have no business wardrobe. I work from home, sprawled in robe or sportswear in front of the TV or the laptop.)

'Would you listen to this lying asshole?' Sammy said, nodding towards the TV, some politician being interviewed on CBC.

'Mommy swore.' Walt said this matter-of-factly, unscandalised.

'You look nice. Got a meeting on today?'

'Advertisers lunch. Pain in the ass.'

'Again.' Walt.

'Any luck?' Sammy said softly, raising her eyebrows. She'd been watching me out there with the cellphone. I shook my head.

'Any luck with what?' Walt asked.

'Do we need anything?' I said, ignoring him, opening the fridge, the gleaming Sub-Zero. 'I'm gonna take a run in to town this afternoon. Thought I'd pick up some fish or something for dinner and –'

'There's those duck breasts in there,' Sammy said, pulling her coat on now. 'Some wild rice in

JOHN NIVEN

the cupboard. Might be nice.' Sammy the editor, always editing.

'Any luck with what?'

'Have you checked the roads?'

'They're fine. Christ, you worry, Donnie.'

This was true. Over fifteen years out here and it still shocked me that Canadians routinely drove through weather that would have brought the army onto the streets of Britain.

'*Any luck with what?*' Walt said for the third time.

'Nothing! Christ, Walt, if –' I checked myself. 'Look, maybe Herby's in the house somewhere, eh? Having a wee sleep. I'll look again after you're at school.'

'He'll turn up, sweetie,' Sammy said. 'C'mere . . .' She knelt to embrace him, her car keys in one hand. 'Daddy's going to look *everywhere*, isn't he?'

'Yeah,' I said, Sammy and I exchanging a look behind Walt's back.

'OK, see you boys tonight,' Sammy said, straightening up. 'Remember, we need that review by lunchtime.'

'Yes, boss.'

She leaned in to peck me on the cheek and whispered close to my ear, 'Check all the outbuildings and call the neighbours again, huh?'

I nodded and clapped my hands, turning to Walt.

'Come on then, trooper. Front and centre right now or we're gonna miss your bus.'

Looking back now, the sheer normality of that weekday morning – the three of us in the kitchen with our goodbyes, our last-minute instructions and half-eaten toast – seems utterly blissful.

2

WALT AND I waved to Sammy's anthracite Range Rover as it vanished around the grove of pine trees at the bottom of the drive before we turned and took the path that ran along the woods bordering the Franklin place; the short cut we always used to get down to the bus stop on Tamora. Our Caterpillar boots crump-crumped through the ankle-deep snow, our breath wreathing behind us, the air so crystalline that breathing it in pierced your lungs sharply. Walt's hot little hand in mine, snowdrifts stretching out ahead of us to the horizon.

I'd drifted here too. Scotland, then England, then Toronto, then on to Saskatchewan. Heading further north and west, further, always further away from home. Huge and landlocked, a long, rectangular slab of prairie land covering over 200,000 square miles but with only a million or so inhabitants,

Saskatchewan contained the population of Birmingham spread over an area more than twice the size of Great Britain. Head south from Regina or Moosejaw and you're soon into America — Montana and North Dakota. To the north — the gleaming icescapes of the Northwest Territories, subarctic once you get much further north than Prince Albert, where Canada's coldest ever temperature was recorded: minus fifty-seven.

'Land of Living Skies' the licence plates say here. The skies didn't seem to me to be living so much as endless. I felt tiny and irrelevant beneath them, like plankton, like krill in the fathomless Atlantic that now separated me from home. Sometimes, in the summers after I first moved here, before I met Sammy, I'd drive out of Regina into the country, heading north towards Saskatoon in the ancient Nissan I'd bought. I'd pull off the road, onto the dusty verge, and lie on the bonnet in the warm Chinook wind, surrounded by wheat fields or cattle, gazing up into those rolling clouds, knowing that if I kept going north for long enough the wheat fields and the cattle and the Chinook winds would all gradually disappear, giving way to the nothingness of the Northwest Territories. Beyond that, Greenland. The Arctic itself. The lemmings, musk ox and caribou. The North Pole. Permafrost. Oblivion.

I'd lie there with the thin car bonnet rippling and buckling beneath me, the metal warm through my shirt. I'd lie there and look north.

Later Sammy told me about the Inuit, the fearsome tribes of hunter-warriors who made their home in the tundra. They'd lived untroubled by the modern world until after the Second World War. Then we arrived, bringing the things we bring: the booze and the substances and the TV. Now much of what was left of the Inuit lived in housing projects in Nuuk, Greenland's capital, doing battle with depression and alcoholism and drug addiction.

Sammy said that the Inuit once believed that suicide purified the soul and made it ready for its journey to the afterworld. That the elderly who had become a burden upon the tribe would often request permission to take their own lives. They had to ask three times and family members could try to dissuade them but, at the third time of asking, the request had to be complied with. They would turn their clothes inside out, bring their possessions to be destroyed, and hang themselves in public. I often wondered about that third conversation. About the look on someone's face when their mother or father approached them and began it. Listening, head inclined, knowing that the request now had to be acceded to.

I became aware that Walt was tugging at my hand, expecting an answer to something. 'Sorry, Walt?'

'I said, are you going to say the movie was good, Dad?'

Walt had only recently started experimenting with 'Dad', with the shortened form, and I was shocked at how diminished I felt when he used it, how grown-up those three letters made him sound and how old they made me feel. The loss of innocence they represented. I missed 'Daddy'. Mommy was still always 'Mommy'.

'Uh, yeah. I guess so.'

'You really liked it?' Walt was talking about the movie we'd watched the night before; a DVD release I had to review for the paper: a hundred-million-dollar riot of fight sequences, implausibility and wooden dialogue. He'd loved it, despite finding the climactic battle a bit traumatic.

'No, Walt, not really.'

His brow furrowed, like his mother's, as he thought about this contradiction. 'How come?'

I thought about the film, about its garish, sickening riot of colour, about how every inch of the screen had been filled to overloading. About its cardboard acting and howling exposition. 'Um,' I said, 'I guess I didn't really like the characters.'

I remember putting an arm around Walt to guide him up a couple of icy steps, onto a higher plane of ground. *This was when you noticed it for the first time. Out of the corner of your left eye. The splash of colour. The hopping birds.*

'So,' Walt said, still looking puzzled, 'how come you're going to say it was good?'

'Well . . .' How to explain the adult world of lies and compromise to an eight-year-old? The *Regina Advertiser*, the paper I wrote for and his mother edited, belonged to that branch of journalism that was basically an advertorial-cum-local-news service. The stories the paper ran were heavily regionally biased: the hockey teams, state political and financial affairs and human interest stories. (On the day Obama was elected the front-page leader was a story about a big government incentive for livestock farmers, with 'NEW US PRESIDENT!' crammed into a quarter-page box on the lower right.) How to tell him that the paper depended on the goodwill of the press offices of the studios who provided the review copies of the DVDs and the tickets to screenings and junkets in Calgary and Toronto? Who organised for me occasional phone interviews with B-list movie stars that would be buffed up into breathless 'Star speaks exclusively to the *Advertiser*!' features that shamelessly plugged whatever movie the star was selling. That, in short, the *Advertiser* was not the *New York Times* and I was not Pauline Kael at the peak of her powers.

'Mommy's paper doesn't really print bad reviews of anything, Walt.'

He thought about this for a moment. 'So you're *lying?*'

'It's not a very big lie, Walt.'

'Didn't you like the bit where —'

Walt went on, watching his feet, talking to the snow, but I wasn't listening any more.

There was a patch of red in the endless white, about twenty yards to my left, surrounded by three strutting crows, headmasterly in their black cloaks, wings like arms stiffly folded behind their backs.

'And then the bit when they attack the —'

Walt hadn't seen. I looked up ahead, we were nearly at the main road now, and saw Jan Franklin's car parked there, the powder-blue BMW, Jan inside with her two boys, Ted and Andy, waiting for the bus, which was coming up Tamora, black and yellow against white.

'Come on, Walt!' I yelled suddenly. 'There's the bus!' Playfully I scooped him up, turning him away from the slick of red, burying his face into my neck, Walt laughing as I ran the last stretch to the bus stop. The Franklin boys were getting out the car now, waving and shouting. I dropped him down and nuzzled a kiss as he ran to join his friends as the bus pulled up. Panting, hands on my hips, I waved to Jan as she pulled off. 'See you later!' I called after Walt and then he was gone, vanishing into the bus.

I waited a moment, waving, before I walked back, the crows flapping unhurriedly into the sky as I approached, settling down thirty or forty yards away to watch me.

I had to stuff a fist into my mouth to keep from yelling out. Herby lay on his back in a circle of blood; the blood had melted into the snow, turning it pink. He had been . . . eviscerated.

The dog's hairless belly had been torn open from its genitals to its chin and the wound seemed to have been prised open, his ribcage snapped apart, the bones jutting skywards like the pipes of some mad organ. Entrails had been torn loose from the belly cavity and ran away into the snow. My gloved hand still in my mouth, fighting tears and nausea, I moved around to the head. The sockets were black and empty, fringed with blood – the crows had taken his eyes – and his teeth were clamped shut in a ferocious, agonised snarl, the tongue hanging out between them by a sliver, like he'd bitten it off in agony. I stumbled and collapsed, falling to my knees in the snow, my legs gone, shaking.

Suddenly the dog moved – his back left leg juddering and kicking. I scrambled backwards in terror.

A rat's head appeared out of the base of the great tear in the belly, just above the genitals, its whiskers slick with blood as it shook its head in the morning sun. Sick with rage I lashed a boot at it and it jumped clean out of Herby's stomach and darted off, trailing gore behind it.

I rolled over and it all came up, the toast and coffee sour and burning in my throat, spurting through my nostrils, hot and melting through the snow, spots and stars dancing in my vision as I retched, the sensation of vomiting in the cold open air, the gore-spattered snow, reminding me of something from long ago.

3

WE'RE IN the clearing in the woods with the bucket full of frogs and toads, dozens of them, from the pond up at Foxes Gate, all squirming in the blue plastic bucket, writhing over each other, hopping up, trying to get out. Tiny little frogs no bigger than your thumb, bloated, oily toads the size of a grown-up's fist. Tommy is throwing, kind of bowling, the frogs and toads to Banny, who stands there with a four-by-two cocked like a baseball player. He misses and misses, all three of us pissing ourselves as the bewildered creatures fly through the air, caught star-shaped, silhouetted with limbs spread out against the summer sky.

'Fuck sake, man!' Banny says. 'Chuck them slower!'

And Tommy obliges, softly lobbing one of the biggest, fattest toads underarm. It floats up into

Banny's striking range and he's already swinging the crude bat around hard. He connects and the toad *explodes* in a burst of viscera – showering me, my face streaked with its stinking blood and guts. Tommy and Banny are howling as, blinking, I fall to my knees and start vomiting chocolate and crisps into the warm earth.

Catching my breath I look up and see what is left of the toad a few feet away. The head and front legs are still trying to crawl, trying to pull themselves along. I start retching again and in the background I can still hear them laughing, hear Tommy saying, 'Fuck sake! Did ye see that, man?! He just started boaking his fucking guts up, man!' And I can hear Banny saying, 'Look at the state of ye! Ya fucking fanny, ye!'

'Their early cruelties,' a report would later say, 'were practised upon animals.'

4

I SHOWERED after I'd cleaned up Herby's remains: putting what was left of him into a green tarpaulin and dragging it round to the pool house, shovelling fresh snow over the gory mess so Walt wouldn't see it when he came home later. I hung my head under the stinging needles and the thought ran over and over – What did that?

We often saw deer in the woods and I tried to imagine a stag ripping into Herby's soft belly with sharp antlers. Ludicrous. A bear? But when had there last been a bear around here? Suddenly I latched onto the most likely explanation – wolves. Hadn't Ben Dorian talked a couple of times about the grey wolves that raided the trash cans behind his bar now and then? The same wolves hunters sometimes said they saw running in packs in the high pines during deer season? Wolves. It had to be. I turned my face up into the spuming nozzle and let the water batter against my forehead, my temples, my neck.

After I'd dressed I tried Sammy's office and was told she was in a meeting. I paced the house in jeans and T-shirt, damp and lightly sweating from the shower, and waited for her to call back.

Our house was built five years ago. It was designed by Lewis Foster, Canada's leading contemporary architect, but built to Sammy's exacting specifications: four and a half thousand square feet over two storeys. Upstairs, what is really ground level, five bedrooms, three bathrooms, my office and the kitchen family room are ranged around an enormous central living area. Downstairs, at basement level, there is a games room with a bar, antique pool table, jukebox and table-tennis table, laundry and utility rooms, a vast four-car garage and Sammy's office. The construction is largely dark timber and glass, the glass (and there is lots of it – the glazier's bill alone was well into six figures) with a bluish tint to it, to help combat the prism-bright sunlight that refracts off the snow for half the year.

Outside there is a heated swimming pool with a large poolhouse-cum-workshop and a tennis court. (Southern Saskatchewan's winters are brutal, but its summers are warm and arid, often getting up into the high twenties for much of July and August, the time of pool parties and cookouts.) Several outbuildings remained from the old farmhouse we demolished to build the house; the stables, the old dairy, a potting shed.

We still had the apartment in Regina too: a two-bedroom condo in the redeveloped Warehouse District. The idea was that we'd use it for overnight stays when we went to the theatre, out to dinner, or to the odd Roughriders game. We didn't do much of that stuff though. We turned into homebodies. Sam used the apartment occasionally if she had to work late when the paper went to bed, or if she had an early meeting.

All of this from sitting at home reviewing movies for the local paper? I landed on my feet, you could say. Lucked out. Won the lottery. Whatever expression you want to use.

The phone trilled into life and I actually jumped. I picked up the nearest cordless, the LCD flashing 'SAM OFFICE'.

'So?' Sammy said briskly, in work mode.

'Herby's dead.'

A pause. 'Oh no. Oh shit. *Shit.*'

'I know. I'm sorry.'

'What happened?'

'I found him down by the path, near the bus stop –'

'Fuck, did Walt –'

'No. I managed to distract him. It's . . . something must have attacked him. A wolf or something.'

'A wolf? When did you ever see a wolf near the house?'

'Well, I don't know what else could have . . . it, it was pretty bad, Sam.'

Another long pause. 'What are we going to tell Walt?'

'Christ knows.'

'What did you do with him?'

'I wrapped him up, most of him, in a tarp and put him out in the pool house.'

'Most of him?'

'Like I said, it was pretty bad, Sammy.'

'Oh Jesus, Donnie. Are you OK?'

'Yeah. Just . . . poor dog. You know?'

'Look, you'd better call the police.'

'The police?'

'Yeah. If there's a wolf attacking animals on people's properties they'll need to know about it. The Franklin boys play down there all the time. You better tell them. And Irene.'

'Right, I . . . I'll call them now.'

'OK,' she said, and I could hear the catch in her voice. 'I'm gonna go and have a little cry now.'

'I'll see you tonight. I love you.'

We hung up and I stood there looking out of those blue-tinted windows at the white beyond, thinking about what we were going to tell Walt. As I scanned the treeline fringing our property, I felt a growing sense of unease, as though I could feel the cold grey eyes of a predator still lurking out there, moving silently with sloped shoulders and panting tongue between the icy, dripping branches, its breath smoking in the winter air, blood staining its lips, flecks of meat between its teeth.

I reached for the phone. They say that a child can progressively understand the death of a pet, a grandparent and, finally, a parent. 'Yeah?' I said aloud to the empty house as I thumbed the button for information, for the number for the police station in Alarbus. 'Who the fuck are "they" anyway?'

5

'HECKOFA NICE day, huh?' Officer Robertson said as we walked down the path towards where I found the dog. He'd asked to see that first.

'Yeah, it sure is.' Even after so long out here I still register mild surprise when I hear these Americanisms, Canadianisms, seeping into my speech, when I hear myself asking, say, where the 'washroom' is, rather than the toilet. I still have the accent though, a thick Ayrshire brogue that can get guttural when I am excited or angry. I tried to lose it, I tried very hard to lose it at one point, but it was impossible. It just refused to go.

Robertson was young, early twenties, nearly half my age, with bushy gingery hair spilling from under his peaked cap, his belt heavy with nightstick, flashlight, cuffs and pistol as he negotiated the snowy path. It took him just twenty minutes to get out here. Slow day at Alarbus PD I figured, picturing the three or four cops who worked at the small station fighting to take the call, to ride out here and break up the day. Alarbus was an affluent suburb of Regina; a pet-slaying probably ranked high in the excitement stakes. I used the twenty minutes it took Robertson to get here to write half of my DVD review. (*'This FX-drenched blockbuster that's a thrill ride for all the family.'* It's not a very big lie, Walt . . .)

'OK,' I said as we came up over the rise. 'Right here is where I found him.'

There was still the imprint of Herby's body in the snow, the ring of pink blood.

'Right,' Robertson said, pushing his cap back, sweat on his forehead and his hands on hips as he looked around, gauging the distance from here to the treeline that bordered the Franklins' place. 'Pretty close to the woods. Could be a wolf, like you say. Mind you –' he looked back towards the main road, the bus stop – 'he might have been hit by a vehicle, crawled over here and then, you know, a lot of the injuries would be post-mortem. Birds and rats and what have you.'

'Really?' I thought of Herby's body, about that giant tear up the belly.

'It's possible.'

'Do you get many cases of wolves doing this kind of stuff?'

'Now and then. More in summer though. This time of year they tend to stay up in the mountains. There was a fella killed by one north of here, about, ooh, three or four years ago? A hunter. Up toward Saskatoon. But it's . . . you know, it's pretty rare.' Robertson bent down, looking at something. He got a pocketknife out and dug in the snow, spearing something. He held up one of the dog's kidneys.

'Oh Jeez,' I said.

'Shame,' he said, straightening back up, letting the kidney fall back into the snow. 'Well, I guess we'd better go take a look at the animal, huh?'

'Yeah. He's out back in the workshop. We can go through the house. Would you like some coffee, Officer?'

'I'd love some coffee.'

We started the trudge back through the snow. 'I have to say,' Robertson said, 'heckofa nice place you got here, Mr Miller. Heckofa nice.'

'Thanks.'

'And your wife's the newspaper editor?'

'That's right.' *Here it comes . . .*

'Which would make Sam Myers your father-in-law?'

'Yep,' I said.

29

Robertson gave a low whistle that contained awe, admiration and a definite undercurrent of 'you poor bastard'.

'Yep,' I said again and we both laughed.

Old Sam. About the only man with balls enough to name his *daughter* after him. There weren't many people in the province who hadn't heard of Sam Myers.

My father-in-law was the textbook self-made man. A real working-class hero. Born dirt poor he'd made his first few million in construction back in the late 1970s. His seed money had helped build Regina's first retail mall on the outskirts of town. Then another. A decade or so later, when the city centre was dying on the vine because all the retail business had followed Old Sam's money out to the suburbs, he started buying up cheap property downtown, which he redeveloped into condominiums like our apartment in the Warehouse District. He got rich at both ends. In the meantime he got into local media, buying up the *Advertiser* in the late eighties, right about the time Sammy graduated with her journalism degree.

She didn't want to work for the old man at first. Went off and cut her teeth doing crime reporting on the *Calgary Star*. She was good too. But in the end the old man begged her, offered her crazy money and the chance to become editor by the time she was thirty. Sammy made a real go of the job though, overcoming the prejudices of a lot of hard-nosed subs and section editors in the process. She upped the circulation by 20 per cent over five years and dragged the paper out of the eighties and into the new technology of the nineties, hiring and firing quite a bit in the process.

I met Sammy at the college in Regina, back in 1998, where I was a mature student on the journalism programme. I'd been in Canada maybe five years then, Toronto first, then out here in Saskatchewan. Sammy came to talk to my class. Even though she was only a few years older than me she seemed impossibly sophisticated and assured, a real journalist, someone living the life I was aspiring to. She talked about the realities of writing for a local daily paper, about what makes a good story, about the role of the subs and the editor. She was good too; funny and self-deprecating.

After her talk, during the coffee and biscuits meet and greet, I'd awkwardly, embarrassedly, asked if I could maybe send her a sample of my work. (*She told you months later, in bed, that she'd liked you right away because you were so unpushy, you didn't seem to think you were the reincarnation of Tom Wolfe like so many other students she'd met.*) She gave me her email address and was patient with my overwritten, adjective-spattered copy. Soon we were both inserting little jokes and did-you-read this? did you see that? things into the emails. Pretty soon we were emailing each other the gags without any copy attached. She started me on the review section; books, DVDs, records.

The first kiss – in the bar across from the office.

Meeting the parents. 'Christ,' I said as we came up the drive in Sammy's car that night. Coming up that drive seemed to take a very long time. Lakeview, the Myers family home, was a fourteen-bedroom Edwardian mansion, hidden behind a grove of elm trees. The only buildings of similar proportions I'd ever visited had been hotels or colleges. 'Don't be intimidated,' Sammy said, pecking my cheek as she rang the doorbell.

It had been hard not to be. The four of us ate in an oak-panelled dining room, sitting around one end of a table that would comfortably have seated ten more people. The maid brought in the courses and I tried to appear worldly and relaxed amid the flickering candles, the leaded crystal and the heavy flatware.

But Old Sam had been charm personified during dinner, even more so later, when we sat by the fire in his study with the decanter of single malt. ('A

Scotsman should appreciate this,' he'd said, handing me a tumbler that must have weighed two pounds. I could have washed my hands in it.) He'd grilled me lightly about my background, my family back home, what had brought me to Toronto, then to Saskatchewan. He'd even asked my 29-year-old advice about a radio station he was thinking of buying. It felt pleasant and convivial enough, it didn't feel like what it really was: an interrogation.

Later, much later, I would realise that Old Sam had used the information I'd given him that night to look into my backstory pretty thoroughly. Indeed, he looked into it as thoroughly as you could look into the backstory of Donald R. Miller.

Which is to say, only so far.

Robertson and I took our coffee through the house and down the path towards the pool area, a couple of hundred yards away from the main house. The pool house was a low one-storey stone building, split into two halves: a changing room with showers, toilets and pine benches, and a workshop/ storage space for gardening machinery, outdoor stuff and sports equipment. We came into the workshop half; an old barbecue set, the big petrol lawnmower Danny the gardener used in summer, an assortment of footballs and baseball bats, racks on the walls holding tools. There, on top of the chest freezer in the corner, was the green tarp containing what was left of Herby. It was very cold in there, our breath steaming as Robertson set his coffee down and lifted back the tarp. I looked away, fixing on a spot on the cinder-block wall as he gave a low whistle through his teeth.

'Oh boy. Yeah. Really, uh, did a number on the poor thing, huh?'

'Yeah. So, you think a wolf? Or wolves?'

'Well, yeah. Or maybe a vehicle, but, it's . . . Jeez. Oh boy.'

He dropped the tarp back over Herby and – unable to help myself – I looked down and caught one last terrible glimpse of the dog's face: those empty black sockets rimmed with red, blood matted into his golden hair. 'Well, I guess I'd better notify neighbouring properties of the incident. Tell them to be careful of pets and children.'

We shook hands as he got into the prowler. 'I meant to ask you, which part of Scotland are you from?'

'Oh, a little place near Glasgow.'

'I got relatives over there myself. Motherwell. You ever been there?'

'Once or twice.'

'I keep meaning to get over and visit, but you know how it is. You get back there much yourself?'

'No. Not much.'

I watched the car disappear into the trees and then reappear a moment later down on Tamora. The sun was brilliant, high in the sky now, and a bead of light flashed golden along the side of the police car as it turned the bend and vanished. From somewhere far off came the sound of a bandsaw, carrying on the still air. Someone cutting wood. Preparing for winter.

6

HERE WE come, the fucking lads, walking down the main corridor during break time: me, Derek Bannerman – Big Banny – and Tommy McKendrick. Ma best buds. Ma true muckers. Hundreds o' kids standing about – Ravenscroft was a big school – eating sweets, drinking ginger. Some wee first years walked past us. Targets. Fucking targets, man, scared wee rabbits in a field o' lions. Tommy flung a leg out and just tripped one of them over, sending his books flying. We pished ourselves. We were only in second year; Tommy and me were thirteen and Banny was fourteen. He'd got held back a year. But he was a big kid, one of those fourteen-year-olds that looked like a man nearly. He'd even got served in the Boot one night. Half the third and fourth years shat it from Banny. He was mental. Every cunt knew this.

'Ho,' Banny nudged me. 'Check it oot.'

There, over in a corner by the noticeboard outside the assembly hall, reading a poster, trying to look invisible, was Craig Docherty.

The fucking Professor himself.

Lord Anthony Parka zipped up all the way. Specs. Even had the fucking uniform on: tie, the lot. His Adidas bag clean, un-graffitied. No 'Madness' or 'The Jam' or 'Skinz' scrawled all over it. Always the first to answer in class. Top of the class for everything. Lived in a massive house on Kilwinning Road. 'Bought houses' we called them. 'Spam Valley,' my dad said, meaning that the idiots who bought their own houses, rather than renting them from the council, had to eat Spam to afford the mortgages. They had a car too, the Dochertys. You'd sometimes see his mum dropping him off near the school gates. She was classy. Fit. Big blonde. Into amateur dramatics and shite like that. Acted in plays doon the Harbour, at the arts centre. 'Ho, Professor,' we'd shout as she drove off. 'Ah'd ride your maw daft so ah wid. Ride her till the fucken wean pushed me oot.'

The Professor talked differently to us too. He said 'seven', not 'seevin'. 'Trousers', not 'troosers'. 'Jacket', not 'jaykit'. When he was asked a question in class he wouldn't not be listening. Or pretend to have misunderstood. He wouldn't say, 'Whit, Miss?' Or shrug his shoulders and make some daft comment to his pals. (He didn't have any pals.) He'd answer the question. Usually correctly and often with additional, unasked-for information. In break periods he didn't stand around in a semicircle out by the bins, smoking and spitting. He went to the library and read fucking books. His every other word wasn't fuck or cunt. He was neither Celtic nor Rangers. He used words in class that we didn't understand. He didn't attempt to hide or mask his intelligence. His entire character was just a mad, unidentifiable blur to us.

Yes, in almost every way the Professor had been custom-designed for bullying.

To have his books slapped out of his hands.

Cocks and baws drawn on his jotters and bag.

To be given unexpected dead legs and arms.

Five rapid to the coupon.

Booted in the baws.

The Professor had only been at our school for a few months. He'd been at some private school before that. One morning, just a few days after he'd arrived, me and Banny had been walking down the crowded art-class corridor, Banny tipping the powdery dregs of a bag of Quavers into his mouth. The Professor was coming towards us in the opposite direction. As we passed him Banny had turned and, casually, mid-sentence almost, spat a huge mouthful of thick, tangy saliva right into Docherty's face. The Professor's expression as the corridor erupted into laughter . . . it wasn't rage, or shame, or hurt. It was just surprise. Stunned surprise that a world like this existed and that he had to live in it.

And yet Docherty still managed to carry a kind of air about him, an air of, if not exactly confidence, then at least of maybe dignity. As if he knew, as none of us did at that age, that one day all of this would end and he could begin his real life, one lived in sunlight and reason, far away from this terrible place of random cruelty and violence. And perhaps it was this air more than anything else that drove Banny mad.

'C'mon,' Banny said, cutting through the throng towards the Professor now, his thigh muscles straining against the ultra-tight iridescent Sta-Prest trousers, the trousers topped with a black Harrington bomber jacket. *Our* uniform.

Coming up from behind, unseen, Banny brought the flat of his hand up and smacked it into the back of the Professor's head, bouncing his face off the noticeboard, sending his glasses flying. Without a word the Professor bent down to retrieve them as Banny tore the poster he'd been reading off the wall. 'School orchestra?' Banny spat. 'School fucking orchestra? Whit instrument dae ye play then, Professor? The pink fucking oboe, ya bender, ye!' Tommy and I laughed. A few others nearby too. Docherty just swallowed and stood there. Looking past Banny, as if fixing on something in the distance. 'Ho!' Banny said, shoving him. 'Ye hear me, ya poofy wee cunt?'

Docherty nodded.

'Come on then. Tell us ye play the pink oboe.'

Docherty adjusted his glasses, forefinger pushing them back on the bridge of his nose, and said nothing.

Banny grabbed him by the tie and pulled him towards him, towering over him, over a foot taller. 'Docherty, ya fanny, tell every cunt ye play the pink oboe or I'll stuff this fucking leaflet doon yer throat.'

'Leave me alone,' Docherty said, struggling.

'Ya cheeky wee cunt.' Banny smashed the A4 Banda-copied leaflet into Docherty's face and started grinding it into his mouth, holding him down and around the neck.

'Fight!' a couple of people shouted.

'Eat it! Eat it, ya fucking bentshot, ye!' Banny shouted.

'BANNERMAN!'

We turned. Wee Fulton, Adventure Kit Fulton, was striding towards us. The woodwork teacher and a right hard bastard. Called Adventure Kit 'cause of his belt with all his stuff on it; a tape measure, keys, pliers and stuff. Banny dropped the Professor, letting him fall to the ground, as Fulton grabbed Banny by the front of his Harrington. 'Are you OK, Craig?' Fulton asked Docherty.

'Yes, sir.'

'Hey! Hands aff, man!' Banny said, slapping at Fulton's hand. People gasped. Aye, Big Banny was mental right enough, mental enough tae cheek Wee Fulton.

Fulton slapped Banny hard across the face with the back of his hand and squared up to him. 'What did you say, son?' he asked Banny through clenched teeth.

This is how it was, in Scotland, in 1982.

The two of them stared at each other, about equal in height. Silence in the hall. Banny held Fulton's gaze a moment longer and then the bell rang, breaking the tension. Fulton let Banny go, prodding a finger into his chest and said, 'Mr McMahon's office. Now. The rest of you, get to your classes.'

As Banny followed Fulton down the familiar

walk to the headmaster's office I turned and looked the other way. The Professor was already far down the corridor, walking briskly, not looking back, lost in the sea of Harringtons, parkas and duffle coats.

7

AFTER ROBERTSON left I sat in my office and thought for a while about doing some work on my screenplay, the thing I pecked at now and then to tell myself that I wasn't just a two-bit regional movie reviewer, that I had big plans afoot. That some day a major motion picture would be fashioned from my current work in progress: a kind of science-fiction disaster story, set in a dystopian future, a post-apocalyptic world where society has been reduced to almost medieval levels. But I hadn't touched the thing for a couple of weeks and trying to get back into it would be like jumping into a freezing sea. Instead I finished the DVD review, trying to airbrush in a patina of criticism that might survive subediting (*'while some might find the film's exposition a little heavy-handed . . .'*).

My office is basically a glass cube that juts out

of the eastern side of the house, the side that faces towards the Bennett farmhouse about half a mile away, rented by Irene, Mrs Kramer, this past year or so. My desk is up against the glass and I get to watch some incredible sunrises in here. On my desk are framed photographs – of Walt and me, laughing together out by the pool, taken a couple of years ago; one of me and Sammy, both in full evening dress, taken at one of her parents' Christmas parties; one of Walt and Herby when he was a puppy, Walt cuddling the dog, its huge tongue scarfing out of its mouth and almost round its neck. I took this photograph and stuffed it into the top drawer, unable to look at it any more. I toyed with the review, trimming it, cutting and pasting, moving sentences around, reordering paragraphs, until I found myself staring into space, remembering, thinking about Scotland.

I looked up from my desk, catching myself mid-thought, suddenly aware of how much I had been thinking about childhood, dwelling on specific moments and people, rather than in the general way we all think about childhood all the time – it flows through us unceasingly, like blood. Why had I suddenly started doing this? The answer came quickly: *because you found the dog, ripped up like it'd*

been vivisected. Because violence came calling, didn't it?
And, quite before I knew what I was doing, I had
clicked on Firefox and was typing his name into
Google. I read down, expecting nothing. He was
not, after all, a famous man; he'd be nearly seventy
too, and unlikely to be one of the search results I
was looking at now:

Follow PCardew on Twitter . . .
Paul Cardew is on Facebook . . .
Paul Cardew, President of Virginia Loan and
Savings . . .
Share Spotify playlists with Paul Cardew
using . . .

And then, right there at the bottom, the second
to last result on the first page, were the words:
'*Rutherglen man dies in house fire*' and a link to
Glasgow's *Evening Times* website.

My forearm was tense, my hand claw-like as I
clicked on the link, still thinking, still allowing
myself to think, 'There's got to be loads of Paul
Cardews in Glasgow, surely . . .'

The page opening, scrolling down, the red-and-
white *Evening Times* logo unfurling in the top left
and then, below it, the photograph: a silver-haired
man, smiling the smile I remembered so well. The

two-paragraph story was dated from eighteen
months ago and I read it quickly:

> Police, fire and ambulance services were called
> to a blaze on 14 Mount Street, Rutherglen,
> late on Saturday night. The body of retired
> social worker Paul Cardew, aged 66, was
> recovered from the scene. The fire appears to
> have been caused by a cigarette.
>
> Sergeant Malcolm Thompson of Strathclyde
> Fire Brigade said, 'This tragic death is a
> reminder of the dangers of smoking in bed.'
> He went on to say –

I gripped the edge of my desk, the sunshine
suddenly too much, too bright around me. I crossed
the office to the bookshelves and quickly found
what I was looking for – two books, kept side by
side low down. One was a tattered, much read
paperback of Robert Tressell's *The Ragged Trousered
Philanthropists*. The other was much fatter, a
hardback folio of *The Complete Works of William
Shakespeare*, but a cheap copy, the kind found in
discount bookstores all over the world, with a little
triangle cut off the inside bottom of the dust sleeve
where the price had been. It was the kind of book
that would have been bought by someone who had

a love of culture but little money. I opened the Shakespeare at the title page and read the inscription that had been written there in neat copperplate more than twenty years ago.

To Donnie,
You've made me proud. Now make yourself proud.
Best wishes for the future, Paul
28 August 1989

I ran my finger over the words, tracing their outline, remembering. Then I leaned my forearms on the bookcase, buried my face in the den they made, and I wept . . .

* * *

'Hello there,' he said. 'I'm Mr Cardew.'

It was a warm morning, late summer of 1982. I was sitting at a desk in the meeting room of Auchentiber Young Offenders Institute. That desk — chipped grey iron legs, bolted to the floor in case it was used as a weapon, the wood surface an insane tableaux of graffiti, some of it scrawled in ink, some of it carved in, some of it carved and then filled in with ink, some of it dating from the 1960s, all of it screaming 'I was here'.

Skinz, NaZareth, UDA, Rab McPherson takes it up the erse, IRA, Dae ye want a chicken supper, Bobby Sands?, UK Subs, Anarchy, Nigers go home, Stevie 12/3/72, Behind Greenhouse 4.30 if ye want yer cock sucked, Troops out 68, CELTIC, Fuck all Screws, NF.

In one corner someone had written a poem:

Sid is dead
But not for me
Because I know
Sid did it his way

The walls were slate grey, enamel paint over brickwork, chipped here and there, the red brick showing through, the sun coming blinding through the barred windows behind him as he loosened his tie and pulled an orange plastic chair up opposite me. 'A fine day,' he said. 'Archie.' He turned to the guard who was reading the *Daily Record* at the table at the far end of the room. 'Do you think we could have a window open please?'

He was well spoken. Posh. 'Up himself,' my dad would have said. Had a blue folder under his arm and he put it on the desk. He took a pack of cigarettes out – Capstan Full Strength, untipped – and put them on top of the folder. I remember his smell, the aftershave I later found out was Old Spice, mixing with tobacco, mixing with the stale reek of the thousands of cigarettes that had been smoked in this room. Mr Cardew wore a dark suit of a heavy material that even I could tell was old-fashioned. His hair was greying at the temples and slicked back with Brylcreem or something. His face was blotchy, with broken blood vessels around the cheeks and pouched, tired-looking eyes. 'So, William,' he yawned, 'tell me a bit about yourself.'

I remember this very clearly. Because no one had ever asked me to do that before. 'I, me and my pals –' my voice was tiny, quiet – 'we, we . . .' I swallowed.

'No, son.' He leaned forward and tapped the file. 'I know what you did. I meant, tell me about you.'

I looked at him properly for the first time. I could feel my face burning because I didn't really know what he meant. 'What about me?' I said finally.

'Well. What do you like to do? In your free time.'

I stared at the desk. Bob Marley, King Kenny, a cock and baws, its wiry hairs, the three drops of spunk around the tip, a stick woman with a massive pair of tits and a hairy bush, Poofs fuck off . . .

'Dunno,' I said. 'Watch telly. Films and that?'

If Mr Cardew was depressed by the utter vacancy of my response he didn't show it. He just nodded. 'What's your favourite film then?' he said.

I fidgeted. Rubbed my nose. Searching for the right answer. Thinking of the hours, days, weeks, spent round at Banny's with the stack of cassettes on the top-loading VHS: *I Spit on Your Grave, The Boogeyman, The Burning, Friday the 13th, Driller Killer, Cannibal Ferox, The Boys in Company C, The* . . .

'OK,' he laughed. 'Just a film you liked then.'

The . . . What was the one, the one Tommy had wanted to switch off 'cause it was all just 'cunts talking pish'? The one that had been really slow but had turned out to be really good in the end. With the guy from that other fi—

'*The Deer Hunter*,' I said. 'That was good.'

A pause. He nodded, looking impressed. (You were always good at telling them what they wanted to hear.) 'Mmmm,' Mr Cardew said. 'Don't you think it was a little bit Walt Disney?'

I looked at him. I didn't know what he meant. Walt Disney? Like for wee kids? 'I . . . naw. No really,' I said.

'Ach, c'mon.' He leaned forward, clasping his

hands together. 'Everybody in the world is trying to get out of Saigon and your man De Niro not only gets in there but he manages to find his pal in that Russian roulette den no bother at all. Wee bit convenient, wasn't it?'

I'd never had a conversation like this before, about a film. Beyond a teacher telling you what something was about or your pals all going 'I liked the bit where . . .' I didn't know it at the time, I thought we were just talking about a film we'd seen, but I was having my first real critical conversation about a work of drama.

'And what about your reading?' Mr Cardew asked. 'What are you reading in here?'

'Jist the –'

'Just.'

'Eh?'

'The word is "just". Not "jist".'

'Aye, well, just the books they have in the library an that.' The books they had in the prison library – Jim Hunter adventures, tattered James Herberts and Stephen Kings.

'An that?'

'Eh?'

'Do you mean they have other things in addition to books in the library?'

'Er, naw.'

'No.'

'No.'

'Right. So you don't need the "an that". The sentence should end at "the books they have in the library".'

I looked at him. I thought he was mental.

'I can see I've got my work cut out here ...' Mr Cardew said.

'Are you my teacher?' I asked.

'Your social worker, William,' he said, reaching into his jacket pocket. He laid a paperback book on the desk in front of me. It was called *The Ragged Trousered Philanthropists*. I didn't know what that meant. 'But there will also be teaching.'

* * *

I sat there for a long time, my eyes fixed on a point in the snow in the mid-distance. I hadn't thought about Mr Cardew in many years. Before I knew what I was doing I had taken the desk keys from the ceramic Ramones mug and was sliding one into the bottom right-hand drawer of my desk, the one that was always kept locked.

Inside was a nickel-plated Ruger .32 automatic, a gift, an odd sort of house-warming present from Mike Rawls, Old Sam's head of security. '*Come on,*

Donnie, living out there in the ass end of nowhere? You'll sleep better knowing you've got an equaliser tucked away somewhere.' Mike took me out into the woods at the back of our property and gave me a little crash course, blasting at paper targets he'd tacked to tree trunks. Sammy disapproved of the gun and, for safety reasons, I kept the magazine in a separate locked drawer. Sometimes, sitting here during the day in the empty house, trying to work, I'd take the unloaded weapon out of the drawer and childishly point it around, aiming through the glass, zeroing in on rocks, trees and birds, squinting with one eye closed as I squeezed off imaginary rounds, enjoying the heft of 1.2 kilos of lethal metal and plastic in my fist.

I opened the drawer and took the gun out. I opened the other drawer and took the magazine out: eight fat brass slugs nestling in there. I slid the magazine into the butt of the pistol, enjoying the sound and feel of the metal 'snick' as perfectly machined parts locked into place. I put the loaded gun – slightly heavier now – back into the drawer and locked it.

I could not have told you exactly why I was doing this.

As I was running the spellcheck and getting ready to hit 'Send' on the review the doorbell rang. I hit

'Save' instead and wandered over to the nearest intercom. Irene's image was fuzzy and blue-grey on the little video screen and she was looking around self-consciously, as people do when they know there is a camera on them. I thumbed the button and said, 'Hi, Irene. Come on in,' pressing the button to release the front door as I spoke. I wiped my eyes, took a deep breath, and headed for the kitchen.

Irene dabbed at her eyes with her handkerchief. 'That poor dog. That poor, poor dog,' she said again in the syrupy Georgia accent Sammy thinks she exaggerates. 'A wolf?'

'Looks that way. Or maybe a vehicle hit him down on Tamora and he, you know, he got thrown a fair distance. Or crawled a bit, trying to make it home.'

'Oh my.' We were in the kitchen, the little TV still on quietly in the background. 'Mind you, that could be right, Donnie. Sometimes at night I can hear those big trucks down on the main road just *hurtling* along. If he'd got down there in the early hours while it was still dark . . . with the roads a bit icy.'

'Yeah. It's just the . . . the way he was just, ripped up, Irene. It was awful.'

'Oh God. He was such a sweet dog too.'

'Christ knows how Walt's gonna take it.'

'The poor thing. What are you going to tell him?'

'I think we'll just go with the hit-by-a-car thing. It'll be better if he can think he didn't suffer.'

'Yes, absolutely. Oh, I have to say I don't envy you that conversation.'

'I know,' I said, going to rise towards the kettle's whistle.

'No, Donnie, I'll get it,' she said, beating me to it. 'The day you've had so far . . .' She walked over to the stove and took the pluming kettle off the heat, then crossed to the fridge and got the milk out, closing the big brushed-steel door with her hip, already opening the drawer for the spoons. Irene knew where everything was, maybe better than Sammy did.

'Walt and I, just the other day, we were throwing sticks for him over in my yard.'

'I know. It's just . . . horrible.'

'Horrible.' She was pouring boiling water into the coffee pot now.

Irene was in her early sixties, maybe a little younger. Big hair. Coppery red. A real Southern belle back in the day you'd imagine, but far from dainty, a big, strong old girl. You'd see her out front sometimes splitting logs, swinging that big axe. She ran four miles most days in spring and summer. She'd been renting the farmhouse next door for the last year or so, a widow, a painter who'd moved here for the landscapes. Though in truth, the idea of the lonely-old-widow-neighbour who we helped out was reversed: Irene was fiercely independent and did much more for us than we did for her. In addition to the frequent babysitting of Walt (for which she refused all payment), she often gave us extra logs when she split too many and she'd always ask if we needed anything from town if she was going down to Alarbus. She even dropped off a pie for us now and then when she'd been baking, something I thought only happened in the movies these days. She was a transplant just like me and had found the climate hard last winter, her first experience of the Canadian deep freeze.

She came back over, the twin funnels of the mugs trailing their steam across the sunlit kitchen. 'Our dog got run over back home, when I was a little girl.' She sat down opposite me at the big table. 'It was terrible. I swear, I cried for days.'

'Yeah. He's going to take it very hard.'

We sipped our coffee. 'How's your winter preparations going by the way?' I asked, wanting to talk about something beside the dog.

'Better than last year, now I know what to expect.

I mean, I knew it'd be cold of course. I just didn't. . .'

'Yeah, me too the first few years, Irene. Sammy, her family, they all think it's normal. The weather they'll drive through . . .'

'I've got all the screens up. Plumber came out and checked all the pipes last week. Snow chains are already on the car. The weather channel says it's going to start hitting week after next.' She nodded towards the TV.

'Yeah.'

'Oh, while I remember, is Walt's hockey game still on for Saturday? I told him I'd come cheer him on.'

'Yep – 10 a.m. at the school.'

'Grand. And do you still want me to babysit on . . . the fifth, wasn't it?'

'That'd be great. I won't be late. Sammy's going to stay in Regina.'

'She said. It's her parents' party thing, isn't it?'

'Yup,' I sighed. 'The royal summons before the King and Queen take their winter leave of absence.'

'Oh to be that rich!' Irene said.

We drank our coffee and looked out at the total white surrounding us, dazzling in the sunshine through the near 180-degree perspective the wrap-around glass wall of the kitchen afforded. 'My,' she said. 'I can never get over how lovely the view is from in here. You're so lucky, Donnie. I swear, I don't know how you ever get any work done.'

Some of Irene's expressions – those 'Mys' and 'I swears' prefacing her sentences – cracked us up, like stage-play Georgian. Blanche from *Streetcar*. Sammy thought the affectation was perhaps born out of homesickness, a loss of identity out here in the Saskatchewan nowhere.

'Me neither. Oh,' I looked at my watch. 'Speaking of which, I do have a deadline actually.'

'Gosh, of course. Sorry, Donnie. I'll let you get back to it. And you're sure there's nothing I can do to help?'

'No, but thanks anyway, Irene.' We stood up. She was the same height as me, Irene.

'Good luck with Walt tonight. Poor lamb.'

'Yeah,' I sighed. 'Yeah.'

Later that night we told Walt that Herby had been hit by a car and killed and, for a moment, it looked like the lie was going to be a massive own goal. *'But who did it, Daddy?!'* The boy was furious, almost yelling. *'You have to catch them! Get the police! Get Grandpa to help!'* Finally, after we'd explained that it was just one of those things, a terrible accident, that the police couldn't launch a manhunt for the hit-and-run killer of a Labrador, he seemed to absorb the fact, to move from anger to grief. He collapsed into Sammy's chest, sobbing, as we sat either side of him, stroking his hair, Sammy crying too as we reminisced about what a good dog he'd been and how he'd be burying bones in doggie heaven now. (It's not a very big lie, Walt.)

Later I carried him to bed in his Spider-Man pyjamas. Later still Sammy heard him crying again and went in. Walt was sitting up holding a photograph he'd found of him and Herby frolicking by the pool last summer.

'Goddammit,' Sammy said sadly as she came back to bed, handing me the photo. It was hard to look at, the dog gazing at the camera, his tongue lolling out playfully, so far removed from the way it had jutted between his teeth in death. *Almost bitten off. The black holes where his eyes had been.* I shrugged the image away, and other images that it was trying to bring on its heels, and pulled Sammy towards me in the warm bed, the keening wind just audible through the thick glass.

'Is something wrong?' she asked. 'I mean, something else?' I let the book I hadn't been reading slide onto my chest and cleared my throat. I couldn't tell her, not properly. *I am Donald Miller.*

'I had some other bad news today,' I said, not looking at her.

'What?'

'Oh, just a . . . an old tutor of mine, from university, I found out online he died a year or so ago.'

'Oh, I'm sorry. Did you know him well?'

'Not in years. At the time though, he . . . he was a good teacher. I hadn't thought about him in a while and just googled his name today.'

'What made you think of him?'

Childhood. The bloody pipe organ of the dog's ribcage.

'Nothing really. Just a stray thought.'

'What a week,' Sammy sighed, resting her head on my chest, her hair tucked under my chin. I patted her forearm.

'Yeah.'

'How did he die?' Sammy asked, ever the reporter. *Who? Where? How? Why?*

'Just, he was old,' I said. (*The word is 'just'. Not 'jist'.*) 'He was old.'

I lay awake for a long time. This had been the first serious inroad on our happiness in the time we'd been living here. The unsettling thing was that part of me felt like I'd been . . . expecting it. Not this exactly, but something. Some version of the other shoe dropping. It felt like I had been a trespasser in happiness and now my time was up. *You*

*landed on your feet. Won the lottery. The pools. Did you
really think it could last? That karma would allow this
to stand? But you don't believe in karma. Nazi war
criminals in their eighties slumber by the pool in South
America while babies get hit by trucks. Stupid, late-night
thoughts. Tired, overreacting to a pet being killed by some
wild animals. What do you expect, living out here in the
wilderness?* I crawled down deep into the bed, as
close to Sammy as I dared without waking her,
feeling her warmth, the easy rhythm of her breathing.
I held her hand gently while she slept, her coral-
pink nail varnish seeming to glow in the moonlight.

An hour went by. I turned this way and that. No
matter which side I lay on I could feel my heart
beating against the sheets, could hear it in my chest.
I got up and went to the kitchen. I craved liquor
but instead made a mug of camomile tea which I
sipped at the big oak table, looking out into dark,
freezing night.

Outside – the wind, the snow and the darkness.

The current of fear.

Wolves in the pines.

* * *

It was what they'd now call 'a drinking culture'.
People drank. Everyone drank. There was the

Christmas Eve my dad got so drunk he came home in the early hours of Christmas Day, stumbling into the living room where my mum had wrapped and laid out all the presents, and decided he 'fancied a wee sweetie' and started unwrapping presents to try and find a selection box — a collection of several different chocolate bars in a festive package, a staple in any Scottish child's Christmas stocking. (I sometimes try to picture Sammy's expression if she had to watch Walt munching his way through the tonnage of sugar that made up our diet.) We came downstairs a few hours later to find him unconscious underneath the tree; his face smeared with chocolate, unwrapped presents scattered all around him, the desecrated trays of the mangled, broken selection boxes and the splintered chocolate globe of a half-eaten Terry's Chocolate Orange. Then I was crying and my mum was screaming at him, kicking him awake, bawling at each other as I ran upstairs.

And then, by New Year, just a week later, at a neighbour's party, the whole episode already recast as comedy. My dad 'pure steamboats', 'fires intae the wean's sweeties'. 'He's no real so he's no!' Everyone laughing. My mum, drunk too, already gazing half affectionately at him as he shrugged under the indulgent laughter of his pals. 'Steamboats' 'foaming', 'para', 'pished'. The incredible misdeeds excused by the invocation of one of these words. (Again, today, I make the inevitable comparisons and picture the consequences if one of our friends came home on Christmas Eve having drunk ten pints of lager and half a bottle of whisky and proceeded to wreck the living room and open half the kids' presents. The expensive month in rehab that would follow. The tearful, twice-weekly psychologist's appointments for parents and children. The trial separation.)

It was drink too that had made my friendship with Banny and Tommy possible. Banny had battered me on one of our first encounters. I say 'battered', it wasn't a real kicking, nothing like the ones I would routinely see him dole out after we became friends. He just walked past me in the corridor during break time one morning in first year and I made the mistake of looking at him. The inevitable exchange: 'Whit ye fucking looking at, wee man?'

'Nothing.'

Bam. He punched me in the stomach, driving all breath out, crumpling me to the floor. 'Don't be fucken cheeky,' he said over his shoulder as he walked off. Then, the following year, we were thirteen now, at Craig Hamilton's party. He was in the

year above us and he had an 'empty', his parents
having rashly gone on holiday and left a fourteen-
year-old in charge of the house. Thirty or forty
teenagers. Litre bottles of Merrydown cider and
cans of beer and quarter-bottles of Whyte &
Mackay and Smirnoff. I'd drunk three cans of white-
and-gold Skol, was drunk for the first time in my
life really, and a few of us were in the garden when
we saw the bobbing light and heard the whirr of
the spokes – a bicycle coming along the path
towards the house. 'Check it oot,' someone, maybe
Tommy, said. 'It's that fanny Kenny Morrison.' A kid
from another school. I didn't know him, but I saw
from Banny's slowly spreading leer as he watched
the approach of the bike that he didn't like this
kid. 'Let's pelt the cunt wi cans,' Banny said, crushing
an empty green Kestrel tin in his fist. There was
a small vegetable bed beside where we were
standing, drinking and smoking. Bamboo rods had
been placed in rows to support runner beans or
something. In a flash of inspiration I pulled one of
the rods out of the soil. As the bike drew level
the others began their hail of abuse and empty
beer cans. Morrison realised at the last moment
what was happening. He stood up in the saddle
and pumped the pedals, turning the handlebars to
the right, looking to accelerate away from us. I

stepped forward, drew the bamboo rod back behind my shoulder like a javelin and hurled it at his front wheel just as Morrison started to shout back, 'GET IT RIGHT FUCKEN UP YE —' It was a one in a hundred shot — right through the spokes, splintering, the bike stopping as hard as if it had hit a brick wall, Kenny Morrison — the 'Y' in 'YESE' still hanging on his lips — getting thrown right over the handlebars of the big purple Chopper, thrown several yards through the air, smashing down onto the concrete pavement, the bike clattering along behind.

The roar of laughter that erupted behind me.

Everyone was pissing themselves. Everyone. But no one more than Banny. Banny was doubled over, gasping for breath, tears streaming down his cheeks. 'Did . . . did ye see the cunt's face?' Banny coming up and putting his arm around my shoulder. 'Fuck sake, wee man. That wiz no real! A fucken belter!' Morrison now, limping away into the night, pushing his bike, shouting back over his shoulder: 'Youse are aw fucking deed, man!'

Big Banny's arm. Around *my* shoulder.

Today, nearly thirty years later, I still sometimes find myself wondering how things might have been, how differently it might have gone for me, if that bamboo pole had missed its mark. If it had flown harmlessly in front of the bike, or clattered uselessly onto the concrete a few yards behind it. If I'd stumbled home alone that night, instead of going into the brightly lit kitchen, into the grey fug of cigarette smoke and music, to drink the green can of Kestrel Banny presented me with from his own personal carry-out.

'Cheers, wee man.'

'Aye. Cheers, Banny.'

8

IN THE weeks after Herby died we were both more solicitous with Walt. His whims were catered to, his tantrums mollified, even though I sometimes thought we erred on the side of being overindulgent in this area. However, from the moment he was born, Sammy's voice had always been dominant in anything to do with Walt's development. Because she'd earned the role: the tower of parenting books on her bedside table (*Listening to Your Child, A Mother's Work*), the open tabs on her laptop at any given time reading something like, 'YOUR CHILD'S DIET', 'SLEEPING PATTERNS', 'REWARDS & PUNISHMENTS'.

And our life went on. Our life whose routines, still, sometimes, when I stepped outside of them and looked with the eyes of childhood, seemed fantastical to me.

The PTA meetings and bake sales. The dinner parties and school fund-raisers. (The last fund-raiser for Walt's school, an auction, raised over forty thousand dollars towards a new library. From a little over a hundred couples – an average spend of a few hundred bucks a head. Sammy scribbled a cheque for two thousand dollars, the furled chequebook flattened on her knee. On the drive home I tried to imagine this happening at the school I went to. I did the mental arithmetic, trying to make sense of the sums: following the maxim – oft repeated to me by Sammy's father – that, a non-hyper rate of inflation being allowed, money roughly halves in value every fifteen years or so, the two thousand Canadian dollars would have been worth a thousand back in the mid-nineties. Back in the late seventies it would have been around five hundred dollars, roughly two hundred pounds given the exchange rate at the time. I tried to imagine my parents writing a cheque to my school for two hundred pounds. This involved imagining my parents having a current account, picturing, say, my mother's handwriting on the actual cheque, her random spelling, her childlike mixture of upper and lower cases – 'TWO HunnDreD pouNDs OwNly' – spilling across the lines. The incredible ceremony the procedure and the sum involved would have occasioned. I kept picturing other family members – uncles, aunts – standing solemnly around the table while the cheque was written, perhaps taking a photograph. I don't often smile when I think about those days, but I smiled that night.)

At these events we mingled with other 'heavy hitters' from Regina and its suburbs. With Ray Glad, the newsreader from CBKT, and his lawyer wife Charlie. With the Becks, Alan, the CEO from Federated Co-op, the oil company, and his wife Hope, a 'homemaker'. With the Saskatchewan Roughriders linebacker Jimmy Treme and his wife Gail. Sammy, with her editorship and a lifetime of her father's money behind her, would float through these occasions, flattening a hand on her breastbone as she dipped her head to listen conspiratorially among the glassware and soft light. Covering her teeth as she laughed at an indiscretion or an aside. People knew who I was because of Sammy or, more rarely, because they recognised me from the postage-stamp-sized photograph that accompanied my byline every week. And they'd ask me things like 'Hey, have you seen this-or-that movie yet?' Or, 'Man, I loved that show too.' Occasionally someone would try and find out about a real estate deal Old Sam was rumoured to be planning ('Hey,

I'm hearing your father-in-law's buying up land around North Central . . .') but, basically, I'd be the guy in the corner eating all the dip. The guy nodding and saying 'Really?' and 'Oh yeah' and 'Jeez!'

The guy wondering if they were all really thinking *'Here comes the househusband. The homemaker.'*

And the talk at these events, of the children. Always about the children: nannies and tutors and doctors. Medications and diet and, even, psychiatrists. Conversations about future colleges for our eight-year-olds.

The children who were chauffeured everywhere, perched high in heavy, burnished 4x4s, swathed in designer casuals, frowning at their BlackBerries and iPhones as they were driven to sleepovers, to their little league hockey games. To play dates and birthday parties at the imposing, remote houses scattered around Alarbus, or in the Crescents area of Regina, that wedge of affluence just north of Wascana Creek. Sometimes, at the birthday parties, the two groups combined: the children in the huge den or basement rec room with their video games, apps and websites, the adults in the kitchen with the Sauvignon Blanc, with the Pouilly-Fumé and the canapés. The kitchens and dens were all very like ours: vast expanses of reclaimed wood and local stone filled with gadgetry: the industrial dish-washers, the hidden Sub-Zeros, the taps that dispensed instant boiling water. All the things we didn't know how we'd managed without. And not too much of that good white wine either – no one really drank. Everyone drove. Everyone had careers. Everyone had *kids*.

I found it difficult, moving among these men, with their talk of stocks and bonds, IPOs and gold prices. Their talk of margins and portfolios and returns. We had all this stuff, of course. We did all this stuff. Or, rather, Sammy did. Quarterly or so she'd attend meetings downtown at Baker and Kenning, the family accountants. Things would be moved around, tax positions strengthened, assets protected. She never talked to me about this stuff and I didn't resent it. What did I have to contribute here? These were people who'd grown up with money. Who felt perfectly comfortable having lots of it and were perfectly sure that the money they had would only bring them lots more. What financial wisdom had I grown up with? I could remember my Uncle Bert, Bert with the tracheotomy, who had only vowels at his disposal, telling me once that 'an ound in oor ocket is oor est end'. *A pound in your pocket is your best friend*. For me reading the financial pages was . . . Mandarin. Sanskrit.

So when, at these gatherings, amid the granite or solid oak kitchen worktops, when talk turned that way and the guys started saying, 'You should really be thinking about this,' or 'You should get your guy to get you in on this,' I'd nod along and sip my drink and say, 'Yeah?' or 'Yeah.' Or 'Yeah, I heard about that.' Or 'Interesting.' And then I'd quickly find an excuse to drift away, off to the side, to go and check on the kids, or nibble at the buffet. Yes, 'margins' was about right. On the margins. Always on the margins.

I loved Sammy and Walt with everything within me. But sometimes, watching them at one of these parent-and-kid gatherings, watching Sammy laughing a little too eagerly or noisily, watching Walt's bored expression, his face glazed, coated with the grey glow from the screen of the phone or video game, I would have the 'Once in a Lifetime' moment (*'You may find yourself . . .'*) and I would think to myself . . . what, exactly?

I read a passage in John Updike recently, in *Rabbit at Rest*, where Harry Angstrom is watching an aeroplane landing that contains his son and grand-children. 'He imagines the plane exploding as it touches down, ignited by one of its glints, in a ball of red flame shadowed in black like you see on TV all the time, and he is shocked to find within himself, imagining this, not much emotion, just a cold thrill at being a witness, a kind of bleak wonder at the fury of chemicals, and relief that he hadn't been on the plane himself . . .'

I had studied Updike on the American Literature module of my degree course and remembered buying the book in hardback when it came out in 1990. (The great, hesitant outlay of fourteen pounds in the student union bookshop. Just over thirty quid in today's money by Old Sam's . . .) I had certainly read these words before, in my early twenties. Rereading them twenty years later they sent a terrifying flash of recognition through me, the urge known to every family man in early-middle age, no matter how good the hand that has been dealt, how agreeable the life. Why this one? ('*How did I get here?*') And the accompanying urge – pale and transitory, never to be realised, but real all the same – to somehow wipe it all away and start again.

And, during those weeks, over November and into December, the winter was bearing down, sharpening every day, the temperature seeing its most severe fall of the year, dropping from around ten degrees at the end of October to minus fifteen by the beginning of December. The average snow-fall for the area during the month of December was nearly two feet, and they were saying it was

going to be a whole lot worse than that this year.
Danny the gardener and handyman checked the
winterising on all the outbuildings. He fitted the
heavy snow chains onto our cars; Sammy's Range
Rover, my Audi. In the skies to the north you could
see great grey knots twisting and flexing, could
feel the air getting heavier and denser, like it was
already made of snow, but you just couldn't see it
yet.

9

'JESUS CHRIST, Walt, *that's enough*!' I said, slamming my palm against the steering wheel, surprising myself with the ferocity of the outburst. I knew without turning that Sammy's eyes were already coolly upon me from the passenger seat. I felt Walt kick my seat from behind and I gripped the wheel tighter, keeping my eyes on the road, the black ribbon slicing through the white surrounding us on all sides, Alarbus high school coming up on our right now through the flaky, powdery snow. I glanced in the rear-view and could see Walt looking out the window, biting his lip, his large brown eyes luminous, shining with unreleased tears.

'I said "we'll see", Walt,' Sammy said quietly.

'See? What is there to see?' I said. 'He's completely irresponsible with things.'

That morning I'd been walking through the

kitchen when I noticed Walt's smartphone, a Samsung Android, lying on top of his jacket on one of the stools by the breakfast counter. The screen was smashed, crystallised into a honeycomb. It was the second phone in less than a year to have gone this way. 'Walt.' I held the phone up. 'What happened this time?'

'It wasn't my fault,' Walt countered automatically. He was bent over his huge red-and-white kitbag, packing in pads, ice skates, his hockey stick leaning against the glass windows behind him.

'It's never your fault,' I said. 'What happened?' I was holding the phone now, tracing the pad of my thumb across the screen. It still seemed to work.

'Danny pushed me in the play—'

'Well, you're just gonna have to live with this, Walt.'

'I can upgrade to a new phone next month anyway.'

Something in me protested, kicked out, at an eight-year-old using the word 'upgrade'. At the casual entitlement of the way that 'anyway' was tossed out. 'For free?' I asked.

'Yeah. Well, no. It . . . it'll cost maybe a hundred dollars.'

'Then that's too bad, buddy,' I said. 'You're going to keep this one for at least another year.'

'But Mom said —'

'I don't care wh—'

Sammy came into the kitchen at this point.

'Have you seen this?' I said, holding the phone up. Sammy sighed, nodding. 'This is the second phone in six months. Well, he's just going to have to live with it.'

'The screen's cracked, Donnie, he'll cut himself.'

I had, indeed, just pricked my thumb with a tiny shard of glass, a pinhead of blood forming. 'We've got some clear tape somewhere,' I said. 'We'll just tape the screen up.'

'*Mom!*' Walt whined.

'Or there's an old Nokia of mine in my office somewhere. He can put his SIM card in that and use it till —'

'A *Nokia?*' Walt said.

'Look, we're going to be late for the game,' Sammy said. 'Can we please discuss this later?'

But I didn't. I kept right at it in the car until I wound up shouting and banging my fist off the steering wheel. We pulled into the parking lot and Walt had the door open and slammed behind him and was running off to meet his friends before I'd even turned the engine off. All around us parents were unloading their eight-year-olds, the boys clambering out of Benzes, Audis and BMW 4x4s laden with kitbags and hockey sticks. I was aware that my heart was pounding.

'What's your problem?' Sammy said, the instant the door closed.

'*My* problem?' I said. 'You're kidding me, right? That fucking phone cost four hundred dollars. He hasn't even had it a year. He's got to learn a . . . a sense of responsibility.'

'He's eight, Donnie.'

'Exactly. I don't even know why an eight-year-old needs a fucking phone like that. He —'

Sammy sighed. This was old ground.

She had recently told me a story about one of Walt's school friends, a fat, freckled kid called Grady. A few months back Grady had gone over his thirty-dollar-a-month cellphone call plan by *six hundred dollars*. The parents had read him the riot act and the dad had taken him off the call plan and put him onto a pay-as-you-go contract. The kid had complained to the mum that he was forever running out of credit and couldn't make calls and what if an emergency came up and he couldn't call them and all the usual bullshit. So, without telling the dad, the mum had put him back on the call plan. The kid had promptly gone nuts with the websites and the chat rooms and Christ knows what and had run up a seven-hundred-dollar bill.

'Seven hundred dollars in a month?' I'd asked.

'Yep,' Sammy had laughed.

I'd tried. I'd really tried to picture my dad's reaction to this news. His face as he was told he'd have to find four-hundred-odd pounds to cover a phone bill his eight-year-old kid had run up. I couldn't do it. I just couldn't even conceive of the scenario. 'So what happened?' I'd asked Sammy. She'd just shrugged in what-can-you-do fashion.

Sammy sat for a moment looking out the window at the other cars, at the exhaust fumes billowing in the freezing air, kids jumping down with their kit. 'We haven't got time for this now,' she said, tugging the door handle. It closed with a heavy, expensive thunk behind her. I sighed and followed.

Junior hockey was huge in the province. Kids learned to skate not long after they could walk. Today Walt's team, the Alarbus Eagles, were playing the Saskatoon Blades. A league game. We filed into the hockey auditorium at the back of the high school. There were already dozens of parents crowded into the bleachers on each side of the rink, wearing North Face jackets in black, red and navy. Gore-tex and Timberland boots. It wasn't much warmer in here than it was outside and the steam rose from their mouths, from their styrofoam coffee cups, misting in the air above them.

There were coolers packed with sandwiches, lite beers and potato chips. Parents stood chatting in groups and Sammy and I returned waves and hellos as we made our way to our seats on the home side, next to Jan Franklin, the Marshes and the Krugers. On the ice the boys were already warming up, testing the surface, streaking back and forth. The wet slap of stick on puck. 'Baby Elephant Walk' rising and falling idiotically in the background.

We'd had an ice rink in our town, at the Leisure Centre, a huge edifice of white-painted corrugated steel that also housed a swimming pool, indoor bowling greens and basketball and squash courts. A cinema too. It was built near the harbour in the late seventies, when I was around Walt's age. I never learned to skate though; I'd hobble round the side, clinging onto the barrier, my rented plastic skates – Purple Panthers we called them – splaying and juttering out from under me as the harder, older boys screamed by on their Bauer Huggers, sending icy jets of water spraying at those of us clinging on, the music booming, deafeningly loud in the huge, cold space: ELO's 'Mr Blue Sky' and Elvis Costello's 'Oliver's Army'. Slush Puppies and Space Invaders and Asteroids.

Banny was among the skaters, although I only

knew him by reputation then. A hard kid in a hard town. I remember watching him speeding past, skating backwards sometimes as he talked to girls, building up speed before twirling to a halt and body-checking some kid, sending them tumbling across the freezing wet ice. I looked out across the bleachers, at the sea of Abercrombie & Fitch. Of Ralph Lauren and Hollister. I couldn't help but think of all the tribes that roamed the halls of my school, back before everyone looked the same.

Mods. Punks. Rockers. Skins. The heavy metallers with their denim waistcoats over their biker jackets. Their patches that said Judas Priest, Saxon and Iron Maiden, Eddie's skeletal features sometimes skilfully emblazoned on the back. The reek of patchouli oil. Goth hadn't really hit our school yet, though there were a couple of kids in the fifth year with black clothes and spiked dyed black hair, their canvas knapsacks emblazoned with strange band names like Bauhaus, the Birthday Party and Alien Sex Fiend. Having younger parents Banny had more interest in fashion than me or Tommy. He'd been somewhere between mod and skin when we first met. A parka, but with close-cropped hair, rather than the Weller crop. Desert boots with Sta-Prest trousers. More recently he was veering towards what we called 'casual': waffle sweaters, slip-on shoes with white socks, stonewashed jeans, Harrington jacket and his hair starting to fall into a

wedge that hung over his right eye. He'd blow the hair
up out of his face when he talked to you.

I realised someone was speaking to me.

'Uh? Sorry . . .'

I turned and looked up to see Irene. Sammy was
standing, talking to the Krugers behind us. 'Hi,
Donnie.'

'Oh, hi, Irene. Sorry – miles away.'

'Is this OK?' She was gesturing to the empty
seat beside me. 'Of course, here . . .' I moved our
coats and scarves and Irene sat down, untying her
scarf and slipping off her parka, her thick red hair
spilling out. Irene was always very precisely made
up – foundation, mascara, lipstick and hair just so
– and perfumed. Her scent was filling the cold air
around me now. She often came to Walt's home
games, a gesture of local support and solidarity
that, I suspected, was more due to simple loneli-
ness: a widow with an entire weekend stretching
emptily ahead of her.

'Brrr,' she said, rubbing her hands together.
'Where's our boy then?' I pointed Walt out.
'Everything OK?' Irene asked. 'You seem a bit
distracted.'

'Oh, I'm fine, just . . .' I glanced to my right;
Sammy's ass was a few feet from my face, she was
deep in conversation with Stephanie Kruger about

something. 'I don't know, Irene. Kids these days . . . they seem to think they can have anything they −' I stopped myself. '*Kids these days*? Christ, listen to me.'

Irene laughed. 'I see. You think you're starting to sound like an old-timer?'

I watched Walt talking to a couple of his friends, sticks cradled in front of them, their hands in the big padded gloves, like the fists of Transformers, of armoured samurai warriors. For a second I had a keen wave of regret for having spoken so harshly to him just before a game and had to fight back the urge to make my way down to rinkside and wish him good luck. The boys were already getting to the age when a parent approaching them when they were with their friends was becoming a source of embarrassment.

'Well, I *am* an old-timer,' Irene said. 'And to be fair, kids nowadays, not just Walt, all of them, they do seem to get an awful lot of expensive stuff. I'll bet it wasn't like that back in Scotland when you were growing up.'

'You're kidding?' I said. 'When I was Walt's age?' I laughed now. 'Nothing like it.'

'Mind you, with all that lovely scenery you wouldn't have needed much, huh? I'd just love to visit there some day.' She fingered her brooch, the word 'just' coming out as 'jest'.

'Oh yeah, we just played in the scenery all the time Irene. It was all you needed.'

I laughed, marvelling at the cliché of how Americans often thought Scotland was one endless, beautifully shot tourist-board ad – the Kyle of Lochalsh joining onto some Hebridean beaches, joining onto Glencoe or whatever – and thought of my home town, of the brown pebble-dash council estates built after the war and already tired by the time I was born in the late sixties. Of the empty prefab factory units next to the bypass, the all-night garage, the sawmill and the rough pubs that dotted the high street. Of the millions of tons of poured concrete that surrounded the place: the roundabouts, ringroads and bypasses designed to get you quickly and smoothly around it and on north towards Glasgow, towards better places.

'Are you mocking me, Donnie?' She was smiling, pretending to be scandalised.

'No, sorry. It's just . . . most of Scotland isn't quite like how people picture it.'

The buzzer rang, signalling the start of the game and the two teams sailed forward across the ice towards each other. Walt skated backwards, taking up his position in defence, to the right of the goal. 'Right, come on, Eagles!' Sammy said, clapping her hands together as she took her seat next to me. 'Oh, hi, Irene! Sorry, didn't see you there.'

'Morning, Sammy.'

'Listen, Stephanie's borrowing our samovar,' Sammy said, turning her attention to me. 'I said you'd take it over tomorrow during the day.'

'Our?' I turned and looked round at Stephanie Kruger, smiling at me in the row behind. 'Just leave it on the porch if we're not in, Donnie,' she said. 'Thanks.'

'It's in the garage somewhere,' Sammy said.

'Well, tomorrow, I –'

She looked at me.

'Fine,' I said. 'No problem.'

I still had the car keys in my hand and I dug the point into my palm as the ref blew his whistle. With a clatter of sticks and a scraping of blades, the game lurched into life below us.

10

THAT NIGHT, after Walt was down, we cooked and ate in the kitchen, a simple pasta-and-salad supper, me draining the pasta and stirring in homemade pesto while Sammy sliced cherry tomatoes in half and added them to a bowl of watercress and rocket. Sammy was a good cook, but meticulous, everything seemed to take hours. Like many women she cleaned as she went along, each spoon and bowl rinsed and placed in the dishwasher, every surface and chopping board wiped clean, any unused ingredients neatly put away. I was faster, but I left in my wake a reeking Passchendaele of crockery, a medieval battlefield of spiralling peelings and bloodied cutlery. When Sammy finished cooking the aromas were the only way you'd know she'd been there.

We ate in silence, Sammy turning the pages of a magazine, me half watching the news on the little

TV, the sound down low. As soon as she'd finished her last mouthful of salad and dabbed a spot of olive oil from her lips with her napkin Sammy looked up and said, 'So, what was all that about today?'

'Huh?' I put my fork down.

'Laying into Walt.'

'I didn't "lay into" him.'

'You're kidding, right? He was really upset. And right before his game too. Nice.'

This was how Sammy did it. She bided her time. Pushed the anger way down deep and chose her moment, usually much later when you had long thought it was over and she'd had time to prepare.

'Oh Jesus. Look, he's got to learn to have more respect for his things. He just –'

'I mean, after all he's been through this past few weeks with Herby and everything.'

'So what are we meant to do when he breaks and loses stuff all the time? Just say, "That's fine, son"? "No problem"? "Here's a cheque"? What kind of message is that sending?'

'It's just a phone. You need to pick your battles.'

'I've heard that one before, Sammy. It seems to me we don't pick any. And besides, that phone cost –'

'Christ,' she said, raising her voice for the first

time. 'You can't keep gauging what Walt should have against what you used to have, Donnie.'

I looked at her. 'What's that supposed to mean?'

'It's late,' she said, getting up.

There was a moment right there when I could have let it go. Where I could have said, 'Sorry for shouting at him.' And it would have been over. But I didn't. I said, 'If anyone should be pissed off about today it should be me.'

She looked at me expectantly, arms folded, weight on one hip.

'Volunteering me to run that thing over to the Krugers' place without even asking me?'

'What's the big deal?'

'It's half an hour away. It'll be an hour and a half out of my day.'

'I didn't know you were that busy.'

Was there anything in this? I looked at her. 'It'd be nice to be asked, rather than be treated like, like a fucking . . . I don't know . . .'

'I just didn't think you'd mind. You often go in to Alarbus in the afternoons, it's on the way. If it's too much trouble I'll call Stephanie and tell her they'll have to pick it up.'

'No, it's fine. I'll do it.' I picked up the TV remote.

'Christ, don't sulk, Donnie.'

'I'm not sulking.'

'Fine. Whatever. I'm going to bed.'

I sat channel-hopping for a while before I turned the TV off and walked the long hallway down to my office. I didn't turn the lights on, there was enough moonlight coming through the three walls of glass to see by. I unlocked the bottom drawer, rooted in below a printout of my screenplay (my own notes scribbled in the margins in red: 'NO!' and 'WHY?') and fished out a bottle of single malt whisky – a 25-year-old Talisker, a Christmas gift from Sammy's dad a couple of years back. There was a glass on the desk with a couple of inches of tepid mineral water in it. I tipped the water into my bin and poured a big glug of the pale whisky. I held the glass under my nose for a moment, the strong fumes making my eyes tear, before I took a drink, gratefully feeling the burn, feeling my face flush and my blood elevate. The whisky had come all the way from Skye, less than a couple of hundred miles north along the west coast from where I grew up. I had never been there. '25 Years of Age'. Made in 1986.

Mr Cardew's nicotine-yellowed fingers as they turned the pages; pointing out certain phrases he'd underlined. Asking you what you thought. Seeing if you were under-standing everything.

JOHN NIVEN

It had been a strange and unexpected thing, coming to love books in my late teens. My father never read anything outside of his tabloid. My mother would occasionally be caught frowning over a dog-eared potboiler lent to her by a friend, or some bodice-ripper she'd borrowed from the library; its lurid covers encased in clear, protective plastic. There had been no books in the house I'd grown up in. As for school, well, the only kids who read books for pleasure, who read outside of when a teacher was literally standing over them in the classroom, were the freaks. The kids like . . . like him. Docherty. The Professor. Strange and unexpected then when I discovered under Mr Cardew's encouragement that what seemed to me to be tracts of boredom and torture actually contained unimaginable vistas, entire worlds of escape. (*And you were much in need of escape then, weren't you?*) That you could open one of them and start turning the pages and that, instead of time slowing down and refusing to pass, you would look up at the clock (*that clock, in its mesh cage*) and the deadly, endless afternoon ahead of you would have vanished.

I thought of Robert Louis Stevenson's 'The Scotsman's Return From Abroad', where Stevenson says 'The king o' drinks, as I conceive it, Talisker, Isla, or Glenlivet!'

What had you said? '*Rather than be treated like, like a fucking . . . I don't know . . .*' But you did know. 'A fucking errand boy.' That had been the phrase forming on your lips. But to say it out loud was to make it real and neither of you wanted that. No – you definitely didn't want that. This Scotsman wouldn't be returning home. Ever.

* * *

The last time I saw my mother was late November 1982, the height of the trial and all the publicity. It was sleeting outside and it had taken her a train and two buses to get there. Her face was wet and her coat steamed gently in the institutional heat of the visitors' room. We sat under the merciless strip lighting and shared the bar of chocolate she had brought me.

'He's not been keeping well,' she'd said by way of explaining my dad's absence. 'And there's been some trouble.' Her lip was trembling as she nibbled on a square of Dairy Milk.

'What trouble?'

'A man . . . a man punched him in the street the other day.' She darted a look at me. Before I could ask 'Why?' she said, 'Because you were his son.'

She started crying softly, her head bowed as she

spoke, almost hiccuping the words out between the sobs. 'The things they're saying in the paper, the things they say you and yer pals did tae that boy. Are they . . . did ye?'

I stared at the floor, numb, and didn't reply.

'Oh, William. Oh, God help ye. God help ye . . .' She kept repeating that. Over and over.

A few weeks later, just before Christmas, I got a package with some presents (a jumper, a pack of playing cards, an Airfix kit) and a letter. The letter was short and written in my mother's strange mixture of upper and lower cases. It said:

Dear William,

MerrY Xmas. Here's a coupLe of Wee presENts. Its no much. Munies a bit tite.

ThiS is a Sad letter to wriTe son. Your Dad and Me have decided we woN't see yoU anymore. WhAt you've dun is Too bad for us too take. I hOpe God Will forGive you BUT we cant. I'll try and remember You as the nice wee Boy you used to bEe and noT who it says you are in the PaPer. I'll always think about YE but you are No lONger a son of ours.

I,m SoRRy,

Mum x

I never saw nor heard from them again. I was thirteen.

* * *

I drained the glass and put the bottle back in the drawer, locking it. As I stood up to leave I saw a light was still on in Irene's house, a yellow square in darkness, about half a mile away. A shadow loomed near it for a second and then, just as I had noticed it, the light went off and the horizon was black.

I went to bed.

11

THERE WERE a couple of hundred guests moving through the large, well-lit rooms of the mansion on Elm Street, the men in black ties, the women in gowns. White-jacketed waiters pressed through the throng topping up glasses from frosted champagne bottles, the bottles smart too in their white neckerchiefs. There were ice sculptures in the hall and a string quartet in the drawing room. I was in my traditional position near the buffet, nibbling on crudités and drinking club soda. (Soda water we called it back home. For many years after I moved out here I thought club soda was a special non-alcoholic cocktail unique to the bar or 'club' you were in. Like the 'house' soda.) This was very much Sammy's environment.

In the last few years, ostensibly to help with her mother's arthritis but, I thought, really, simply to enjoy their wealth, Sammy's parents had begun decamping to Hawaii around the middle of every December, to a suite in the Ritz-Carlton on Maui, overlooking pineapple fields and the sea. They stayed there until the beginning of March, missing the absolute worst of the Canadian winter. We usually flew out a few days before Christmas and spent a fortnight with them, coming home right after New Year's. Old Sam had taken to throwing a big Christmas party at the house before they went and now the occasion was set in stone. It was a good chance to schmooze advertisers, the Mayor and the like. I was spearing a shrimp when I heard a deep voice behind me saying, 'Hitting the hard stuff, huh?'

'Hi, Mike,' I said, turning. Mike Rawls, Old Sam's security chief – six three, two hundred plus pounds – was grinning and nodding towards my brimming tumbler of clear, bubbly water.

'Driving home later.'

'That'll make us the only two sober people here then.'

We stood and surveyed the crush, Mike doing so with the practised eye of someone used to scanning crowds for trouble; for someone getting too close, moving too quickly, or staring too intensely. 'Hey,' he said, 'sorry to hear about your dog.'

'Ah, yeah.'

'What happened exactly?'

I told him the whole story, having gotten it down to a routine pitch. 'It was horrible. Just ripped the poor bastard to pieces. The policeman even found a kidney in the snow. They're going to —'

'That's odd, huh?' Mike said.

'What's odd?'

'Well, you'd think it'd be one of the first things they'd eat, wouldn't you? A pack of hungry wolves? The kidneys, the liver, the sweetbreads? Anyway —' Mike raised a hand to another security guy who was signalling him from the main door across the hallway — 'I gotta run. I think the Governor's arriving. Catch you later, Donnie.'

I watched him go and suddenly I had the urge to check on Walt. I headed for the back garden, passing through the drawing room where the string quartet were starting *The Four Seasons* again, taking out my cellphone and dialling as I went. Irene answered on the third ring, just as I stepped out onto the back porch, into the freezing December air, shivering in my tuxedo.

'Hi there, Donnie. How's the party?'

'It's fine. I'm about ready to leave. How's Walt?'

'He's fine. We've been playing his video game thingy. He's just about to go to bed, aren't you,

Walt?' I heard some kind of protest in the background. 'Don't rush home on our account.'

'No, I've done my thing here. Shown my face. Can I talk to him?' A muffled fumbling and then Walt's voice on the line. 'Hi, Dad.'

'Hey, son, how's things?'

'OK. I beat Irene at Medal of Honour!'

'Did you? I'm sure that's not really Irene's thing.'

'She's pretty good. Better than you!'

'Really? Well, look, it's nine thirty. Time for bed.'

'When are you coming home?'

'In about an hour or so. But you'll be asleep by then, won't you?'

'Yes, Dad.' He says this automatically, dutifully.

'OK. Sleep well. Night, son.'

I hung up and looked out over the trees. The air was so sharp now that to inhale was to feel a stinging burn on the rims of your nostrils, a wintry crackling in your lungs. The black sky felt heavy above me, like it was swollen with the impending snow.

You'd think it'd be one of the first things they'd eat, wouldn't you?

I heard the door opening behind me and turned to see the old man himself coming out, a thick coat over his shoulders and a great cigar clamped between his teeth and already lit, his cheeks

97

bullfrogging as he puffed, getting it going, grey, perfumed smoke wreathing his bald head. 'Donnie,' he said simply, nodding.

'Hi, Sam.' I held up the cellphone by way of explanation for what I was doing out here, feeling, as I often felt in Sam Sr's presence, that I had been caught doing something inappropriate. 'Just checking in on Walt.'

'How is the little fella?'

'He's fine. Just off to bed.' I remembered now how Walt's first instinct when we told him about Herby had been to try and get the old man to do something. *Get Grandpa to . . .*

'Want one?' Old Sam said, patting his pocket, holding up the cigar.

'No, I'm good. Some party. I hear the Governor's here.'

'Yeah,' he yawned, stretching, looking at his watch. 'Took his time getting here too. I'm gonna have to kick all these freeloading bums out soon.' The old man was in his late sixties now but in good shape, lean and trim, the hair loss the only concession to ageing. Hard, clear eyes, the kind you wouldn't want to look into and bullshit. I'd once seen a drunk at a restaurant downtown get too mouthy, too familiar with Sam, and he'd knocked the guy out. Clean. One punch. He'd had to pay the guy off in the end, of course. 'You get your picture in the paper now and then,' he said afterwards, 'people figure they can say anything to you.'

'What time are you getting off tomorrow?' I asked.

'Five fifty in the a.m. Chopper to Winnipeg then the flight to LA.'

'You want to get to bed, Sam.'

'Ah, you don't need too much sleep at my age.' He puffed on his cigar and we stood looking out over the lawn, the elms, the moonlight as the party thrummed in the house behind us, the hum of conversation, the music. 'Might be last time we throw one of these,' he said.

'How come?'

'Well, I'm nearly seventy, Donnie. You start to think in terms of "lasts".'

'Christ, Sam, you've another –'

'Ah.' He cut off whatever platitude I was about to utter with a wave of the cigar.

'Well,' I said, yawning myself now. 'I'd better go find Sammy. Say goodnight. I'm driving back.'

He nodded. 'And Walt's coping OK with the dog business?'

'I think so. He's a bit shaken up. We all are.'

'Damn shame. Anyway, you'd better get a move on if you're driving, look . . .' I followed his pointing, glowing cigar tip and saw that, behind me, the snow had started falling silently in huge powdery flakes.

'Bang on cue,' I said. 'Well, thanks for the party.'

'And we'll see you all on the island in a few days?'

'Twenty-second,' I said.

'Night, Donnie.' We shook hands. 'Drive safe.'

I found Sammy in the lounge, near the great fireplace, talking to Billy Vaughan, the paper's Head of Advertising, and what looked like a gathering of favoured clients, middle-aged guys in tuxedos holding Scotches. Sammy was wearing a long black dress that clung to her, deeply décolleté, with a little diamond brooch, her hair down tonight, spilling over her shoulders. In her heels she towered over most of the men. She was in mid-sentence as I approached, saying the words, '. . . to drive more traffic to the website . . .' I smiled at her and she said, 'Excuse me a second, guys.' Billy took up her speech as she came towards me, taking a few steps away from the group. *The kept man.*

'I'm gonna take off.'

'Really?' Sammy said. 'It's only –' She looked at her watch. 'Shit.'

'Yeah, time flies when you're hanging with the big boys.'

She made a face and whispered, 'I'm bored shit-less listening to myself and my feet are killing me.'

'That's why you get the big bucks, baby.' A line I used often. 'Anyway, I want to get going before the snow gets any heavier.'

'OK. I'll – Hi, Graham,' she said to a passing tuxedo. 'I'll see you tomorrow. Give Walt a big kiss from me.'

'Yep.' I leaned in to peck her quickly on the cheek. Sammy wasn't big on public displays of affection.

'Drive safe.' She turned and walked back off towards the fireplace. I watched her go, roughly hitching up one of the spaghetti shoulder straps of her dress with a thumb as she went, always some-thing of the tomboy, the jock, about Sammy.

I got my overcoat, the valet brought the car round, and I headed down the drive, the heater cranked full, snowflakes whirring through the cones of the headlights. The great Edwardian house disappeared behind me, its many windows blazing with light in the rear-view mirror.

12

THE HOUSE I grew up in. Post-war pebble-dash. Woodchip walls and sworling, nicotine-baked Artex on the ceilings; the pine mantelpiece with its knick-knacks, geegaws and ornaments, the multicoloured glass clown, the glazed ceramic horse tiredly pulling its cartload of barrels, the white ashtray with Blackpool Tower etched into its base in gold; the squat television encased in plastic wood; the electric fire with its fake coals, glowing a soft tangerine on winter nights, pitch dark at four thirty as I lay on the carpet watching *Roobarb and Custard*, or *Magpie*, my face burning and my back freezing, icy pools of condensation on the windowsills.

They both drank, my parents. My dad openly, my mum more secretly. My dad worked in the timber yard. They'd finish work at 4 p.m. and go to the King's or the Delta. Two hours in there, five or six pints, and home for his tea. Then the steady stream of cans of Tennent's in front of the television until he passed out around ten. By the time he got in from the pub my mum would have been on the Martinis, not Martinis as I came to know them in later life, after I met Sammy – the chilled stem glass, the clear gin and the bobbing olive – just sweet vermouth with lemonade. She'd start on these in the late afternoon, keeping the bottle out of sight in the pantry, glugging them in the kitchen while she sweated over the frying pan and the boiling potatoes. By teatime she'd some-times have put away half a bottle or more and the tea would be burnt or cold and the fights would start. One night, staggering, swaying, she dropped the plate into his lap accidentally, spattering hot fat over him. He smashed the plate to pieces off the wall and punched her in the stomach, screaming 'YA STEAMING FUCKING MESS, YE!' while I ran crying for my room. Later she came up, drunker, and told me they'd just had a 'wee argument', that it was all fine. I'd get the odd slap, punch or kick, but I didn't really get hit. (I mean, I didn't get hit like Banny got hit.) My dad lost his job in 1981, when the timber yard closed down, like so much else in Ayrshire around then ('that fucken hoor

Thatcher') and the drinking and the fighting intensified in that last year I spent at home. My mum
got a part-time job cleaning offices and my dad
would go to the bookies, or do the odd day on
building sites, his visits to the Delta or the King's
getting earlier, three o'clock, two o'clock.

Now I can see that my parents disliked each
other and perhaps blamed each other for the stag-
nation of their lives. They had no common interests;
in fact, no interests at all; just the endlessly flickering
telly, the pall of cigarette smoke, the silence broken
now and then by the crack and hiss of a ring pull,
a stilted conversation about something in the local
newspaper. Locked in this sad battle, they barely
noticed me and I came and went as I pleased. Later,
much later, one of the therapists would suggest
that, unable to break through to my parents, I went
elsewhere for attention.

Banny, Tommy and me did the usual stuff. We
smashed windows. We raided people's gardens.
Our friendship intensified over that hot, endless,
Royal Wedding summer. Having watched the riots
in Toxteth and Brixton on the telly, having seen
those burning orange petrol bombs flying through
the dark, we stole a length of rubber hose from
chemistry class and went out one night siphoning
petrol out of cars into empty milk bottles. I

remember getting a mouthful of bitter, oily petrol, gagging and retching while Banny and Tommy laughed. We stuffed rags into the bottles and threw them at the wall of the church and watched the flames lick up the white pebble-dash. The burn marks were still there years later. We did that.

I threw the frog off the flyover onto the car below. I trained the airgun on the kid on the bike. I hurled the wee girl's shoes into the pond. I asked the woman in the chippy for a swatch at her vag. I told the teacher to fuck off. And, as I did these things, as I heard the boys laugh and honk their approval. I felt their acceptance. I felt their affectionate gaze.

Yes, I felt their love.

* * *

I put the car in the huge garage, the headlights picking out the towers of packing crates towards the back — old furniture, stuff we never used, earmarked for charity shops and garage sales — and turned the ignition off. I breathed out. I'd felt anxious all the way back, every set of headlights that appeared in my mirror had seemed filled with significance, with menace. Even in the garage now, crossing the chill, empty breeze-block space towards the door that connected with the house, I felt jangled, nervy, fighting the urge to look over my shoulder.

Irene was reading a book in the vast living room, her feet folded up beneath her, and she looked up from her pool of light as I came in. 'Hi, Donnie,' she yawned.

'Hi there. Well, how was he?'

'A little angel. He went down just after you rang. Not a peep since. Were the roads OK? Looks like it's getting pretty heavy out there.'

'Fine really. Gritters were already out.'

I flopped down on the big sofa opposite her, loosening my bow tie.

'And how was the big party this year?' Irene asked, almost girlishly. She figured Sammy and me for local celebrities and I think she found our lives impossibly glamorous. Irene never went anywhere.

I made a face. 'Not my thing really.'

'Who was there?'

'Oh, the usual – politicians and moneymen. Tell you what, I was going to have a little nightcap. Fancy one?'

'Oh, just a ginger ale if you have some.'

'Come on, Irene, live a little.' *That song, the summer of 1982, on the radio all the time, right after it all happened . . .*

She laughed. 'Doesn't agree with me at all, Donnie. You know that.'

I crossed to the full wet bar in the corner: the stainless-steel sink, the little glass-fronted refrigerator for the beers, white wine and soft drinks. I reached in and took out a can of Canada Dry. I opened the double doors of the big drinks cabinet above the sink – row upon row of spirits, everything from amaretto to Campari to several different malt whiskies. Irene whistled behind me. 'My,' she said. 'You could open a liquor store with all that!'

'Yeah, Sammy keeps it well stocked,' I said over my shoulder, pulling the cork from a bottle of Macallan. 'I think she's inherited it from her parents, you know? The kind of people who're used to "entertaining".' I poured a hefty glug of the whisky into a crystal tumbler. The ice bucket was empty. 'Do you want ice, Irene?'

'Oh, don't worry, it'll be fine as is.'

I filled a little jug from the tap, poured a splash of water into my whisky and brought the drinks over. 'Mmmm,' Irene said, sipping hers.

'Cheers,' I said, raising my glass as I sat back down.

'Cheers,' Irene chorused, raising her sugar water. I had noticed over the last year or so, when Irene came over for barbecues, or for dinner occasionally, or to use the pool in summer, that she never drank alcohol, but I'd never asked the question directly before.

'Have you never drunk, Irene?'

'Oh, I've tried it of course. Where I grew up, in Macon? It's bootlegger country. A couple of generations back everybody had a pot still in the yard. Everybody drank back home.'

'Not you though.'

'Well, I just always hated that feeling of losing control, you know? As soon as the room started spinning or you felt yourself getting light-headed, I'd just think "that's enough". And considering it only took me about one drink to get there . . . it didn't really seem worth it.'

'I bet your friends loved you.'

'Huh?'

'Always having a designated driver on hand.'

'Oh yes. That was always me all right!'

I took a long pull on my drink and looked at the wooden beams of the ceiling high above, holding the glass just below my chin, the rich fumes tearing my eyes.

'Does it remind you of home?' Irene asked.

It was my turn to say 'Huh?'

'The whisky?'

'Oh, right. Well, a little bit, I suppose.'

Yeah, right. A fifty-dollar bottle of single malt — that was a regular feature round our way. I thought of the whiskies my father drank — the half- and quarter-bottles of Bell's or Whyte & Mackay. The occasional full bottle of a supermarket's own brand.

I took another long swallow, the alcohol hitting me now, everything slowing and relaxing, the anxiety of the drive, of the last few days, melting away.

'You don't talk much about back home, do you, Donnie?'

'I, uh, I guess I don't. No.'

'I thought you Scots were meant to be ultra patriotic. Always talking about how great the old country was.'

'I suppose they do. I guess because I left so young and I don't have much in the way of family back there . . .'

'Sounds sad,' Irene said.

'Nah. To be honest, I don't really think about it much.' This was true until recently.

'Anyway, you've got your own little family here now.'

'And the extended family,' I said, gesturing to my tux. 'Pain in the ass though they can be at times.' She laughed. There was a pause. I watched the snow blowing by the tall window behind her.

There was another question I'd never asked Irene. Braved by the whisky I went ahead. 'Can I ask, and please don't be offended, but how come you never had children, Irene?'

'Couldn't,' she shrugged. 'Jim and I wanted to. It just never seemed to happen.'

'I'm sorry,' I said, touched by the straightforwardness of her answer. She waved a hand.

'Oh, it was such a long time ago. I suppose today we'd have been in and out of IVF clinics and goodness knows what but back then, the seventies, early eighties, it just seemed more that folks accepted what nature dealt them.'

'You're very good with Walt, you know.'

'Oh, he's a sweet boy.'

'Mmm. When he wants to be.' I looked at my watch. 'Christ, speaking of which the wee bugger'll be up soon enough.'

'Yep, past my bedtime too.' She put the half-drunk glass of ginger ale on a coaster on a side table and we both stood up.

'Thanks again for babysitting.'

'Any time, Donnie.'

I saw her out then walked along the hall to check on Walt. Pausing by the door to his room I looked through the hall window and saw Irene's tail lights vanishing into the snow. Unexpectedly, I felt a little sad and protective towards her, going home alone, to a dark, empty, rented house. I'd talk to Sammy. Make a point of inviting her over for dinner more often. Maybe there was even someone we could introduce her to, a friend of Sammy's parents or something. I'd talk to Sammy.

13

'AWW, DADDY, make pancakes. Please. *Please!*'

The morning after the party, Walt bent over in supplication in the kitchen, almost on his knees, knowing that a plea for this kind of doughy, fried breakfast on a school day would receive short shrift from his mother and that I was more malleable. Behind him the snow was falling steadily through the wall of glass, as it had been all night. I looked at the time on the bottom of the TV screen, next to the rolling news feed (*'oil prices set to hit 150 dollars a barrel, economists say . . .'*) and saw it was 7.32. The bus came at 8.15. 'I . . . shit, OK, Walt. Sit down and drink your juice.'

'Yaayyy!'

I kept an eye on the TV weather while I slapped the small blue Le Creuset pan onto the hob and got the eggs and butter from the fridge. Now, in the morning light of the kitchen, last night's anxiety – the headlights – seemed ridiculous. It was Friday. We had a clear weekend ahead of us: no parties or visits or engagements. *Yaayyy*, as Walt liked to say. We'd hang around the house. Maybe get the snow-mobile out.

I beat an egg into the whisked flour and milk, the pan almost smoking hot now, and turned back to the TV. The weather girl was gesturing at a huge grey cyclone. 'These very strong winds are going to keep pushing south, past Saskatoon and into the Regina area by mid-afternoon, driving this heavy snow into real blizzard conditions . . .'

'Can I have chocolate spread on my –'

'No way, dude. Lemon, OK?'

'Aww.'

The phone rang and I picked up the one on the wall nearest to me, the caller ID saying 'APARTMENT'. 'Hi, Sammy,' I said, reaching for the pan. 'How'd it go – Ahh, fuck!' The pan, already red hot.

'What's wrong?'

'I just burnt myself. Ow!'

'Daddy swore.' Walt, in the background.

'What are you doing?'

'I was just, uh, making us some pancakes.' I was

turning my hand under the cold water now, the phone cradled in my neck.

'Oh, don't give him pancakes, Donnie. Let him have his oatmeal or some —'

'I just, look, if I don't get a move on he won't get any-fucking-thing!'

'Again! Daddy!'

'Sorry! Christ.'

'OK, OK. I was just checking in.'

'Have you seen the forecast by the way?'

'Yeah, I'm watching it now.' I pictured Sammy alone in the apartment, in the open-plan kitchen living room, eating her own oatmeal, watching the same channel I was. 'I'm gonna try and leave around lunchtime. Looks like the worst of it isn't gonna hit us until late afternoon.'

'OK. Look, I gotta run, bus'll be here soon.'

'Give Walt a kiss from me.'

'Drive safe.'

I threw the pan back on the heat, using an oven glove this time, and Walt ate his second pancake in his gloved hand as we struggled through the gently falling snow towards the bus stop. There was no trace of the mess where I'd found Herby. It was all covered by fresh, virgin snow. But the spot still made me feel uneasy.

Back at the house I remembered I had a

saccharine romcom to review for the following week: two big teen stars in what looked like a Jane Austen rewrite with text messaging and iPods. I lay on the sofa for a long time, sipping tea and tapping the DVD against my knee, until I wandered down the hall to my office and stood over the desk, my finger tracing over the smooth plastic pad of the laptop, the cursor hovering briefly over the icon for Mozilla Firefox – that flaming orange-and-white beast encircling the globe, the pathway to Google, the mortal enemy of the stay-at-home writer – before moving along the toolbar and hovering over the Word icon. Fuck it. The review could wait. I slid the cursor further along and clicked on the foresty-green Final Draft logo and, with a heavy sigh, steeling myself, opened UNTITLED.

The last scene I'd been working on had been my first-act climax (falling around page 30 on a 120-page script, all the manuals said), where Welles, the hero, is rooting around in the ruined basement of an office building and he accidentally stumbles upon an ancient laptop, something he has never seen before, that has somehow (and how indeed, I hadn't quite cracked this part yet) retained enough power to be turned on. I noticed that the scene was almost falling on page 40 (I had some fat to trim) and read through what I'd last written: squirming, sighing and occasionally letting out a small cry of pain at a particularly heavy-handed bit of dialogue. I deleted chunks, thought for a moment and then typed:

```
INT. BASEMENT - DAY
It's dark. Shafts of murky
daylight pour through cracks
in the ruined stone. Welles
runs a hand over the strange
object, accidentally hitting
the 'ON' switch. The laptop
suddenly comes to life, the
screen glowing a soft blue,
looking as futuristic and
alien in this world as the
shining obelisk in 2001.
Welles jumps back, astonished.
```

The creative writing MA had convinced me I wanted to do *something* literary with myself, but I was thoroughly terrified by the idea of attempting a novel. Three or four hundred pages? Treading in the footsteps of Joyce, Nabokov and Proust? The screenplay, on the other hand, could be just a hundred or so pages long. With a lot of indented dialogue. And you were treading in the footsteps of, who exactly? Joe Eszterhas? Or the guy who wrote *Earth Girls are Easy*? This seemed less intimidating.

Like many fools before me, I was wrong, of course. Over the last five years, inspired by a stack of screenwriting manuals, I had attempted three scripts, all abandoned somewhere between the first and second drafts. There had been the sci-fi western: a reimagining of *Rio Bravo* set on the hostile moon of a remote planet. ('*Take the essential elements of a classic movie and recast it in a strikingly different setting.*') There was the 'creature feature', a horror about huge prehistoric bugs discovered in a deep, abandoned mineshaft. ('*Good low-budget horror ideas are always very marketable.*') Then there had been the road trip idea about two old college buddies trying to track down their former girlfriends. ('Bromances' seemed to be hot.) What I learned over the course of these disasters was that the screenplay was, in fact, very difficult to write. That the form depended on economy, compression and, most of all, like all forms of fiction, upon the vital throb of energy brought only by injecting the writer's own experience onto the page.

I was a good student in many ways. For years I applied all of the stuff I learned in writing class.

I set aside a specific writing time each day to work. ('The muse is more likely to show up if she knows where you're going to be every day,' Stephen King said.) I understood the importance of William Goldman's aphorism that 'storytelling is structure'. I got Syd Field's 'Know Your Ending!' maxim. Most of all I truly felt David Mamet's observation that artists are driven to 'lessen the burden of the unbearable disparity between their conscious and unconscious minds, and so achieve peace'. But this was where I came up short.

For I found only a void in the place where I needed to speak from. Well, not a void exactly, since it wasn't empty. Rather it was a locked vault, my own basement scene.

I reread the page, deleted most of it, and decided to go in to town for lunch.

14

ALARBUS, SASKATCHEWAN — pop 12,000 — lay six miles south of us, towards Regina. A prosperous town, most of its main street, Quintus Avenue, was lined with bookshops and antique stores, designer boutiques, a Starbucks, a high-end deli where we'd shop for olives and prosciutto, Clarke's the butcher's and Hermann's the stationer's. There was a handful of impressive turn-of-the-century buildings like the bank (now the Grange, a luxury hotel with a steak and seafood restaurant), the old post office and the courthouse.

I went into Hermann's and bought some printer paper and ink cartridges. I went into Starbucks, bought a latte and read the newspaper, the snow falling lightly but constantly now. Shoppers moved through the flakes, coming out of Clarke's with parcels of meat wrapped in paper, browsing in the windows of the antique stores at cherrywood desks and Tiffany lamps. A young couple went by, laughing, the guy wearing a long scarf that was wrapped around both their necks. Cars reversed out and moved off carefully, almost as if they were trembling into motion, coltishly finding their legs in the slush and ice.

I thought about the evening meal. Duck breasts with wild rice and spinach. I could make a sauce by deglazing the pan with a little red wine. Maybe flambé it to finish off – Walt loved it when I did that stuff. Or should I pop into the butcher's and get some bacon or pancetta to wrap the duck in? Thinking about cooking sharpened my appetite – it was after one and I hadn't eaten since those pancakes. Across the street I could see the red-and-blue neon sign that said 'DORIAN'S BAR&GRILL' and, below it, in white, the words 'Home Cooking'.

I hung my coat on the rack and stomped the snow off my boots, already smelling something good. Dorian's was a long, low-ceilinged room with a circular mahogany bar, forty-odd feet in diameter, cutting the room in half. The front part was tables surrounded by fake red leather banquettes. Stained-glass mosaic lampshades hung down over the banquettes, casting greenish pools of light. The back part was a small dance floor with a little stage, a couple of pool tables on the dance floor now, but they moved them away when they had bands on at the weekend. 'Hey, Donnie,' Ben said from behind the brass pumps, pouring a beer as I approached. 'Be right with you.' He took the beer down the bar to a group of regulars who were watching the hockey. I recognised a couple and nodded hello. 'What'll it be?' Ben said, coming back up the bar, wiping his hands on his apron. Ben was in his late sixties and he and his wife Kim had run this place for over thirty years now. 'Since Hitler was a corporal,' he liked to say. Ben had crinkly frost-white hair and wore wire-rimmed glasses. He gave off a kindly, professorial air.

'What's the special?'

'Venison stew. Kim's been simmering five pounds of it in red wine since breakfast.'

'Sold. And, uh . . .' I hesitated, looking at the sodas and juices racked in their chiller. Then back to the brass pumps. 'A beer please, Ben.'

As he worked the tap, without looking up, Ben said, 'We heard about your dog. Damn shame.'

'Yeah. It's been rough on Walt.'

'I'll bet. Wolves right?'

'That's what it looks like.'

'Yeah, we had 'em in our trash cans a few times.

Damn nuisance. Here you go . . .' He handed me the cold, beaded glass. 'Go grab a table if you like, Donnie. I'll bring your food over.'

I rarely drank at lunchtime and just two guilty sips of the beer elevated my blood and had me looking out at snowy Quintus Avenue in a rosy, Christmas light. *Maybe the basement Welles finds the laptop in has some sort of generator that's kept running? Or maybe I don't even need to explain it that thoroughly. Will the audience really question the scene? Maybe it's what Jonathan Demme calls a 'refrigerator moment'. The kind of thing that people watch and then, maybe, a few hours later, when they're at home, opening the fridge to get a soda or something, they say to themselves: 'Hang on a minute, how did . . . ?'* So the laptop just happens to have a tiny charge left in it. So what? I began to feel better about the scene, about the whole premise. Maybe it could work. *His spirits soared, like a drunkard's,* I thought, remembering a line from Plato, or maybe Socrates, that I often thought of when a couple of drinks got me thinking like I imagined a writer thought.

Sammy, a Saskatchewan blueblood, a veteran of boards, charities and committees, had, to some degree, viewed me as a project. Something to nurture, develop and change. The smoking went first. Non-negotiable. Then the drinking was moderated. I came from a place where everyone drank to excess. Sammy came from a place where a third drink was often considered bad form. Drinks were sipped. A glass of wine, maybe two, would span the entire meal. I wasn't, by my reckoning, a heavy drinker, but in the years I'd been on my own I'd developed a routine; the wine with cooking the evening meal, the bottle often finished by the time the meal was ready, opening the second and always finishing it before bed. It helped with the anxiety, the ever-creeping sense of dread around dusk. To Sammy, opening a second bottle of wine constituted a binge. Now I'd sip Diet Coke or sparkling spring water while I cooked, pouring the wine only when we sat down to eat, sometimes allowing myself a second glass. Very rarely, if Sammy was busy and I was clearing up and loading the dishwasher alone, I'd pour myself a third.

I didn't think that I resented any of this. It felt like I succumbed willingly to her programme of improvement. But now and then, when that second glass of wine had worked its way down, setting off an empowering, reckless glow, I'd have the urge to drag the Scotch bottle out of the cupboard and sit drinking it right in front of her. *When we blame our genes we are really blaming ourselves*. But, sometimes, it really was as if I could feel my genes rearing up, feel the DNA flexing in coils inside me and saying *'this is what we want'*.

There had been one or two flashpoints, moments of defiance over the ten years we'd been together. One night I went out with some of the guys from the paper, a few of the subs, some of the other writers, the idea being dinner and home at a reasonable hour. We'd ended up getting drunk in a bar in Regina. Someone had offered me a cigarette and I'd taken it. It had lit a trail of happiness so deep inside of me that I'd wound up smoking a whole pack, coming home in the early hours staggering and reeking of tobacco. Sammy's mood had lasted three days. Three days of near-silent meals, of watching TV in separate rooms after Walt had gone to bed. Of Sammy sleeping as far over on her side of the bed as was possible without toppling onto the floor. On the third night I'd apologised and promised her it would never happen again and things gradually returned to normal.

Then there had been that time in the late spring one year. With the warm weather on the way I'd been down in the pool house and workshop one evening, straightening things out, preparing for the summer, digging out the croquet set. Sammy and Walt were out. I'd been rooting on a high shelf when, inside a toolbox belonging to Danny the gardener, I'd found a half-pint of Canadian Club and a pack of Lucky Strikes, a book of matches tucked into the cellophane of the pack. On a mad impulse I poured a big slug of the whisky into a plastic cup. I knocked half of it back, lit one of the Luckies and sat back on the pine bench in the changing room, feeling the warm, amber burn, the heavenly tang of the nicotine as I watched the dusk gathering over the garden. The smoke caught in brilliant skeins in the last shafts of light streaming through the dusty windows. I poured another, lit another, and lay there for a while until nerves overtook me and I aired the room out before running up the garden to the house, where I showered, changed, doused myself in aftershave and managed to brush my teeth three times before Sammy and Walt came home. 'You smell nice, Daddy,' Walt had said.

The perfect crime.

'Here you go,' Ben said suddenly, from nowhere, snapping me out of it. 'Just like Momma used to make.' He set the bowl in front of me, along with a little wire basket containing condiments and cutlery. 'You need anything else?'

'No, I'm good, thanks, Ben.'

'Enjoy.'

The stew was thick, a deep reddish brown, with

nubs of white potato and green peas floating in among the tender deer meat. Hot steam rising and warming my face. *Like Momma used to make.* I tried to picture my mother dicing carrot, celery, onion and bacon to make a *mirepoix*, pouring a bottle of red wine into five pounds of venison, tasting and seasoning the sauce as it simmered, reducing, and I nearly laughed out loud right there in the quiet bar. No. There was no Proustian rush here for me. The food of my childhood, of provincial Scotland in the 1970s and early 80s: Findus Crispy Pancakes and tinned spaghetti hoops. Mince and tatties and Campbell's Tomato Soup. Birds Eye Potato Waffles – 'they're *waffly versatile*' – and Super Noodles. Trying to picture my mother cooking something like this was ludicrous, beyond imagining. Like trying to picture a TV super-chef reverently working a can opener around the lid of a tinned steak pie.

I laughed.

BANNY'S HOME life made mine look like the Waltons. He was one of the very few kids whose parents were divorced back then. He seemed to come and go between his mum's and his dad's, staying with one until they'd had enough, or it became inconvenient for them, and then he'd get punted back to the other, his brown Adidas bag with its black felt-tip graffiti ('Mods' '1690') slung over his shoulder, walking his swaggering walk, spitting on the ground every ten steps. My home life was sterile and loveless – but there was usually a meal on the table at a regular time, a notional bedtime to be enforced. My clothes got washed. Banny lived on fish and pizza suppers and takeaways from the Chinky. Sometimes, he didn't smell too good.

His parents' divorce was never mentioned. One of the times I saw him go most mental, most berserk, was when Adam Adrian called him a 'bastard' in an argument. 'Bastard' wasn't the worst thing any of us said to each other, but it was out of the ordinary. In our parlance, in our time and place, 'bastard' was something you said if you hurt yourself ('Agh! Bastard!') or if, say, you were aiming an airgun at a plump seagull, or a chattering starling, and missed. 'Ya bastard, ye!' might be what you said as you watched it flap away. 'Bastard' as a direct insult was rare. 'Prick', 'fanny', 'bawbag', 'cunt', 'knob', 'tool'. These were the things we called each other. 'Daft bastard' was used when someone was being slow or thick. But it wasn't 'daft bastard' Adam used that break time, round the back at the bins, passing the smouldering Regals back and forth. I can't remember what the disagreement was about but Adam turned away from Banny and said, venomously, 'Ya fucking *bastard*, ye.'

'Whit did you fucking call me?' Banny said as people took a step back. You could see it on Banny's face; Adam was implying that Banny was a *real* bastard because his parents weren't married. A few minutes later, his nose burst open, his front teeth loose, the just-visible imprint of a Doc Marten sole on his cheek, Adam took it back.

Banny's parents were young. His mum 'up the duff' at fifteen, married just after her sixteenth birthday, the cheap wedding dress swollen with Banny. She'd have been twenty-eight when I met Banny in first year, his dad maybe a year older. Still being in their twenties they did things my parents never did: music blared loudly in their homes late into the night. There were fights and arguments with their neighbours. Parties every weekend. Especially at his dad's flat, where a group of his dad's mates pretty much lived from Friday night until the early hours of Monday morning.

His mum was worse in a way. She'd go off for the night, staying with friends, going to parties, leaving Banny in charge of his little sister, who was eleven. This meant me and Tommy could come and stay over. When you came in the front door you noticed the smell first; damp, like wet digestive biscuits. The carpet was worn down to the shiny underlay in three separate paths: one leading into the kitchen, one to the living room, and one up the stairs. The sheets and blankets on Banny's bed (Tommy and I shared it, he slept in his mum's) were tattered, thin and damp. The house was cold too, even in springtime. There was no central heating, the only warmth coming from three port-able paraffin heaters: two downstairs and one in his mum's bedroom. The first time I stayed the night Banny asked me if I wanted a hot-water bottle. He returned with an Alpine Red Kola bottle filled with boiling water, the glass so hot it couldn't be held anywhere near your bare legs. Tommy and I acknowledged to each other that Banny's house was quite 'bugsy', but, of course, this was never voiced in public.

Banny's mum had a video recorder – one of the first people we knew to own such a thing – and a neighbour, a thin, frail woman called Auld Joan, who would buy your drink, your 'cairry-oot', from the off-licence: a half-bottle of Smirnoff and six green cans of Kestrel lager between the three of us. After a couple of the vodkas mixed with cola or lemonade and a can of the thin, bitter lager, the house seemed warmer and brighter as we settled in to watch *I Spit on Your Grave*, *The Boogeyman*, *The Burning*, or a porno borrowed from Banny's dad, the three of us laughing and joking except for those moments during the porn films when it would get very quiet in the room. Intense. You'd be conscious of the sound of your own breathing, the pulse in your groin. (All these details – the unsupervised teenagers, the drink, the violent and pornographic videos – would be pored over later, at the trial.)

Unlike his mum, who would want rid of us when she was having a 'night with the girls', Banny's dad didn't seem to mind having us around. We called him 'Jim', not Mr Bannerman, the only one of our friends' parents who allowed this. By the time we were thirteen, we were allowed to sit in on some of Jim's parties, allowed to take a few cans from the crates on the kitchen floor, allowed to watch the pornos that played endlessly on the living-room TV. There would sometimes be girls at these parties too, but often it would just be a big gang of lads, plus me, Banny and Tommy.

One night we added a half-bottle of Whyte & Mackay to the few cans we were allowed and got drunk. Steaming. I remember stumbling down the hallway looking for the toilet – looking to be sick, 'Antmusic' by Adam and the Ants coming from the living room, blaring over the roar of conversation, the laughter, the groans from the porno film – when I saw Banny coming out of a bedroom. His eyes were wet, sharp-ringed and fixed straight ahead, and he didn't look at me. As I hurried into the bathroom, one hand clamped over my mouth, the Scotch twisting within me, I saw, out of the corner of my eye, two figures in the darkened bedroom Banny had emerged from. It was glimpsed very briefly as I lurched from the gloom of the hallway into the glaring bathroom, but I was sure one of them was Banny's dad and that what they were doing was straightening up.

Tucking in shirts. Tightening belts.

I never mentioned it to anyone. I came close once, a few weeks later, when Tommy and I spent a rare afternoon alone together, walking down to the puggies. Banny had the flu. We were talking about how hard it was to pee when you had a hard-on.

'Aye, man,' Tommy said. 'Me and Banny were trying tae do that once, up the woods. The mad bastard, he . . .' Tommy trailed off.

'What?' I asked.

'Nothing. Ah cannae mind.'

A moment passed. A few steps. Tommy spat on the pavement.

'Tommy, mind at that party at Banny's dad's a couple o' weeks back? I –' Before I could go on Tommy pointed excitedly to the back doorstep of a house.

'Check it oot, man – there's some ginger bottles lying there! Curries an aw! Two bob a pop!'

And he took off towards the glittering loot.

There was something else too. Something I never even attempted to bring up with Tommy. With anyone.

The camping trip.

The previous August, the last week of the summer holidays, four of us had gone camping. Me,

Banny, Tommy and Alec Hardy. Me and Tommy and Alec had all told our parents we were sleeping over at each other's houses. Banny didn't tell his mum or dad anything. They didn't give a fuck. Alec's folks were into camping and he smuggled their two canvas two-man tents out of the garage, along with the wee gas stove, a couple of battered sauce-pans and a few chipped enamel plates and mugs. Everyone raided the backs of their mums' cupboards for provisions: tins of beans, spaghetti hoops and a few heels of bread. Banny got his mum's mate to buy the carry-out: eight cans of Bass Special and a half-bottle of vodka.

We hiked up over the bypass and through the woods. Then up round the lake and north into the forest. We camped beside a stream – put the tents up and lit a fire.

It was great – we ate the beans and spaghetti hoops around the fire as the late-summer dusk closed in. It felt like we were on the edge of the world, in some remote primitive wilderness, not just in some woods less than a mile from a public park. As it got darker, you could feel an edge of apprehension creeping in, but the crack and hiss of ring pulls soon dispelled that: the lager and the vodka warming our blood, making us feel invincible as we sat around the campfire trying to tell ghost stories, but winding up talking about girls from school, about sex.

'Karen McLintoch?' Alec said. 'Ah fingered her daft at the Christmas disco, man.'

'Did ye fuck!' Tommy said.

'Ah swear oan ma maw's life,' Alec said. 'Mind, Banny? Up the back o' the hall, by the Christmas tree?'

'Who gies a fuck?' said Banny, opening his second beer, the foam running down the can as he brought it quickly to his lips, trying not to waste any. He burped, then said, 'McLintoch's a fucking bike, man. Every cunt's been up her. Ah fucken rode her at Stevie Blair's big brother's party.'

'No way,' Alec said.

'You wantin yer jaw tanned?' Banny said. 'Like I'd make it up about riding that monster?'

'She's a'right,' Tommy said.

'Karen McLintoch?' Banny said. 'She's a coupon like a skelped erse, man.'

'Aye, well, you're the cunt that rode her!' Alec said.

'Too right,' Banny said, standing up. 'Ye don't look at the fucken mantelpiece when yer poking the fire, wee man.' He burped and headed into the bushes, unzipping his fly. The three of us laughed, the usual reflexive, slightly manic laughter that

Banny's jokes were afforded, Tommy slapping his knee and repeating 'Ye don't look at the mantelpiece when yer poking the fire! True enough, man!'

Alec and I looked at each other across the fire. The woodsmoke was stinging my eyes so I couldn't be sure, but Alec had stopped laughing quicker than us and I thought I saw him shaking his head.

I remember taking a gulp of neat vodka that was just a little too much: the sour taste as water seemed to pump from the underside of my tongue, flooding my mouth and then I was stumbling off into the trees, vomit spraying over bushes and tree trunks. The shouts and laughter and jeering of the others and the next thing I knew I was moaning and crawling into one of the tents and passing out.

I woke up in the middle of the night, fully clothed in the sleeping bag, writhing awake from a dream of flesh and sex. It was silent and freezing cold, a faint glow and crackle from the dying campfire outside. I was on my side and I had an erection, a dull, aching pressure in my groin. It took a moment to realise that a hand was inside my jeans, clamped around my cock. I felt breath on my neck and then Banny's voice. 'C'mon,' he whispered, his breath short, urgency in his voice. 'C'mon . . .'

I remember my body going rigid. Stiffening with fear, my heart seeming to stop. I stared into the cold darkness and felt him pressing against me from behind.

I started to cry.

It seemed to take a moment for him to realise what I was doing. A moment before he muttered a disgusted 'Fuck sake, man . . .' He let go of me and rolled away, turning his back. I lay there for a long time, blinking cold tears in the darkness until I finally fell asleep again just before dawn.

It was never mentioned and within a few days I convinced myself that I had dreamt it.

16

BY 4 P.M. that Friday it was already getting dark and I was standing in parka, muffler and boots at the bus stop. The storm was well under way; the snow coming in sideways, so thick I could just make out the orange lights of the school bus as it rattled slowly up the hill towards me. I was jittery, having drunk a big pot of coffee during the afternoon, trying to blast away the sleepy effects of the lunchtime beer.

'Daddy!' Walt yelled as he came carefully down the icy steps towards me, the two Franklin boys behind him. A blast of heat and steam rolled out of the bus behind the kids, Ted the bus driver sitting high up in the brightly lit cab. 'How are the roads?' I asked, raising my voice above the growling diesel.

'Main highways are about passable. Moving real slow. I don't know how much longer you'll be able to get all the way up here, though. This is my last stop.'

'OK, thanks, Ted.'

I got Walt into the house, dried off and sat in front of some cartoons with his snack – milk and toast with peanut butter – and called Sammy's cell, getting only soft, feminine tones telling me *'the person you are trying to reach is currently unavailable'*, the voice smug, almost upbeat, reminding you of the blandly malevolent computers beloved of sci-fi; Mother from *Alien*, Hal from *2001*. I called the office and Kelly, Sammy's PA, picked up.

'Hi, Kelly, is Sammy still there?'

'No. She left before lunch. Said she had to meet someone and she'd probably go straight home. I thought she'd be back by now.'

'Uh, no. I –'. A current of fear.

'Have you tried her cell?'

'Unreachable. Who was she meeting?'

'I don't know, seemed a bit last minute, Donnie. Wasn't in her diary.'

'Right.'

'She's probably just stuck in traffic with no cell signal.'

'OK. Thanks, Kelly. I'll keep trying her.'

'Have a nice weekend.'

'You too.'

I hung up and flipped on the TV, channel-hopping till I got the local weather, the reporter in parka standing in front of a shot of traffic on Highway 10 out of Regina, snow blowing around him, behind him red tail lights as far as you could see one way, white the other as he said, '. . . backed up on Highways 10, 5 and 1. The good news is that most major routes are still open, the gritters are out in force and people should be able to complete their journeys, it's just going to take a little time . . .' I thumbed the sound back down. She was just stuck in that tailback, maybe even in one of the cars in shot. No cell signal because of the weather. Worst-case scenario she'd make it as far as Alarbus tonight and check into the Grange and we'd figure it out in the morning. It'd be fine.

I walked over to the wall of glass and looked out towards the highway, to where a pair of headlights were slowly making their way along the road. They passed the house, becoming red tail lights, then an orange signal started blinking and the car took the next turning along from us. Irene, making it home from wherever she'd been. The roads were still passable then. I checked the clock and saw it was just after five. I decided I might as well start dinner. As I opened the bottle of thick Shiraz and poured myself a glass, I told myself I was going to use some for the sauce anyway, and tried to ignore the voice saying, *'That beer at lunchtime? Wine at five? You're drinking more than you usually do. You're nervous — aren't you?'*

When the rice started to bubble and the oven behind me was hot, I quickly scored the duck breasts with the big Global chef's knife, cutting four lines across each one, through the fat and just into the flesh. I pressed sea salt and Chinese five-spice into each cut and then rubbed a little olive oil over them. While I was doing this the heavy orange grill pan was heating on the front burner, wisps of smoke starting to curl up from its bars. I slapped the duck skin-side down onto the pan and they crackled and hissed, sending smoke up into the chrome hood. I turned the extractor fan on as Walt ambled into the kitchen.

'What's for dinner?'

'Duck, son,' I quack-quacked. 'Here, you can help me.'

'Aww, not peeling garlic!' One of Walt's most hated sous-chef tasks.

'No, relax.' I passed him the steamer that would fit neatly on top of the rice pot and a pound bag of spinach. 'Open that and put the spinach in the steamer.'

Walt looked at the big bag of emerald-green leaves. 'There's only three of us, Dad.'

'I know. It shrinks a lot when you cook it.'

'When's Mommy back?'

'She might be late, with the weather. We'll go ahead and eat first.'

I sipped my wine and watched the boy fumblingly set about his task. 'How was school? Anything happen?'

'Josh Barrett got in trouble again.'

'How come?'

'He's such a douchebag.'

'Walt! Don't say that.'

'How come?'

'I . . . do you even know what it means?'

'Like, an idiot or something?'

'Well, no. It . . . just don't say it, OK?'

Walt thought for a moment, stuffing leaves into the steamer, some spilling onto the counter, the floor. 'Can I say he's a douche?'

'No! You can say . . . doofus.'

'*Doofus*? Christ, Dad.'

'Walt,' I said.

'OK, OK. He's a doofus. What does that even mean?'

'I think it means a cross between stupid and foolish. So what did he do, Josh Hartlett?'

'Josh *Barrett*. Right, OK. Well, you know Miss McGovern doesn't let people eat candy in class? So he . . . no, wait, first Alex Trower said, he —'

And Walt was off, telling his eight-year-old's tale: a monologue of non sequiturs, digressions and asides. Characters would appear randomly and then disappear having had no real bearing on events whatsoever. At the end of his story no conclusions would have been reached and no real information would have been imparted. It was like . . . like reading one of my screenplays.

Half listening, I used long-handled tongs to turn the duck breasts: just four minutes and the skin had crisped nicely. I gave them a couple of minutes on the other side and then transferred them to a roasting tray and put them into the oven. Another five minutes or so in there for medium rare. 'Dad?' Walt was asking me.

'Yeah?'

'Do you think it hurt Herby? When the car hit him?' Walt's voice quiet, not looking up at me, concentrating on the spinach.

I came closer and set my wine down. 'No, son. Probably not. He wouldn't have known anything about it.'

That agonised, teethbared snarl.

'I keep thinking about him.'

'So do I.' I put my hand on his arm. 'That's normal, Walt.'

'Do you think, one day, we can get another dog?'

'Sure.'

He'd almost bitten his tongue off.

'I wouldn't want to call him Herby though.'

'We'll call him whatever you like. Anything but douchebag.' Walt laughed at the forbidden word and, warmed by the wine, I saw an opening. 'Look, Walt, I'm sorry about the other day. For losing my temper over the phone thing.'

'S' OK,' he shrugged.

'I just, when I was a kid . . . . I didn't have things like you do. Sometimes it's hard for me when I see you being so careless. But I shouldn't have shouted at you like that.'

'Did your uncle shout at you when you were little?' Walt only knew the official backstory.

'Sometimes.'

'Were you bad a lot?'

'I guess I could be. Here, gimme that . . .' I took the full steamer and popped it on top of the rice. 'Now watch this.'

I put the grill pan I'd cooked the duck in back on the burner and turned it all the way up till the dry pan was crackling. I tipped a glass of wine in there and it erupted, fizzing and bubbling crazily. I tilted the pan, letting the flames from the burner lick into the liquid, and blue-orange flames leapt a couple of feet up into the air.

'Woah!' Walt laughed.

I blew the flames out and scraped at the bars with a wooden spoon, stirring tiny bits of caramelised duck into the sauce, adding a cube of butter to thicken it further, bringing a glossy shine to it. I reduced the heat and let it bubble gently, reducing. 'OK,' I said, clapping my hands together, 'dinner'll be ready in five minutes. Let's just try your mom again.' I picked up the cordless, hit the speed dial and brought the phone up to my ear. I jerked it away quickly when all I got was a single, shrill tone. I jabbed the button to hang up and released it, getting the same dead tone.

'Shit.'

'What's wrong?'

'I think the phone line might be down.'

'Down where?'

'It means it's broken. Maybe because of the storm.'

I picked up my cell – nothing, not a bar of signal now – and sighed. 'Don't worry. I'm sure Mom's fine.' I reached for the bottle of Shiraz and noticed it was three-quarters empty. I drained it into my glass anyway. 'Come on then. Let's get some plates. How about we eat in front of the TV? Catch a movie?' A rare treat, generally forbidden by Sammy.

'Yaayyy,' Walt said as, behind him, the snow came

down through the dark night and pummelled noiselessly against the thick glass.

Were you bad a lot?

* * *

We didn't talk about the actual crime for a long
time, many months. It was the late winter of '84,
February or early March, the trees outside still bare,
the sky stark and then black by five o'clock, and
we were onto Shakespeare now. Mr Cardew was
not yet Paul, that was still some way off, but we'd
grown comfortable with each other. He had a way
of opening up the parts of myself I had to shut off
to survive in the institute. I see now that he was
showing me that who I was at this time, in this
place, did not have to define who I would become.

We were doing *Macbeth*, for O-level English, and
we'd been reading the scene where Duncan's wife
and baby are killed. I was quiet. He put his book
down, removed his glasses and rubbed his eyes.
'In your own time, William,' he said quietly.

'What?'

'Whatever's on your mind. In your own time.'

I looked at my shoes, the plastic prison shoes,
and spoke softly through the fringe that hung down
covering my face. 'People hate us. Hate me.'

'Who hates you?'

'Everyone. For what we did.'

I peeked up through my fringe. He was chewing on the stem of his glasses, looking away from me. Silence in that sad, grey room. 'Well,' he said after a long time, 'I often find people's capacity to be surprised by the cruelty of children surprising. Look at the situation we just had there in Cambodia. Wee boys with machine guns leading the charge. People want to think you're a monster, William, because that's easy. An easy thing to think.'

'Maybe I am. A monster.'

'"As flies to wanton boys, are we to the gods; They kill us for their sport." It's from another play. *King Lear*. Do you know what "wanton" means, in the sense Shakespeare uses it here?'

I shook my head, fighting tears.

'Cruel. Unjust. Merciless.'

'We didn't mean it.'

He took my head and brought it to his chest as I wept. And I said it for the first time, the thing that had been building in me since I came here, since I got my mum's letter.

'What . . . what's going to happen to me?'

Tobacco and aftershave, the itch of his suit on my cheek as he took my face in his hands and looked into my eyes.

'Listen to me, William. Listen now.' I took deep breaths and controlled the sobbing. 'You did a terrible thing, you and your friends. But you can still grow up to be a good man. And don't let anyone tell you different. Do you understand?'

I just looked at him. He gripped my face tighter and said more urgently, 'Do you understand me, William? This is important.'

I nodded.

'Good boy,' Mr Cardew said.

17

WE ATE our meals – Walt leaving most of the
slithery green spinach leaves, burying them under
rice and cutlery – on trays on our laps in front of
the big TV in the living room, the one that lived
in an armoire, where the doors folded back to
reveal the TV and stereo equipment. (Sammy had
been the first person I'd known who thought it
'tacky' to have a giant TV as the focal point of a
room.) Flipping aimlessly we'd found *Toy Story 3*
about halfway through on one of the movie channels and stayed with it, even though we had it on
DVD anyway. (There is always something more
exciting about discovering a movie already playing
rather than laboriously putting it on yourself.)

I say 'we' watched it but really I was somewhere
else, doing calculations in my head: *Say she had a
long lunch, finished about three, got on the road then,*

normally an hour's drive, say two or even three hours with the weather, she'd be getting into Alarbus about now, she'd maybe try a payphone, but the fucking line's down. Could she send an email from her BlackBerry if she had Wi-Fi? I checked my email on my iPhone – nothing.

I tuned back into the movie, near the end now, the toys all in that huge garbage incinerator, sliding down a slushy mountain of landfill towards the fires of hell, towards certain doom. Solemnly they accept their fate. Tenderly they begin to hold hands, preparing to meet death with dignity and love. Suddenly, inevitably, tears were springing to my eyes and I was pulling Walt towards me on the sofa, folding his little head onto my heaving chest. 'Don't cry, Daddy,' Walt said automatically. 'It's going to be OK.' I cry easily at most films but anything to do with childhood, with inno-cence . . .

Maybe I should just get both of us wrapped up and try and make it over to Irene's and see if her phone's still working. What if she has to spend the night in the car? She'd be OK as long as she could keep the heater running. When did she last fill up the tank? Last night, that's right. On the way to her parents' party, so –

'Daddy?' Walt was sitting up.

'Mmmm?'

'What's that noise?'

I listened. 'What?'

'Listen.'

I thumbed the 'MUTE' button on the remote (on the screen, just as I did this, Lotso Huggin Bear was being picked up by the garbage man: the last image, the last moment, of normality for me) and sat forward. I could hear it now: a deep regular thumping, somewhere outside, somewhere above the house, getting louder as we both stood up and moved towards the huge picture window, looking up into the black sky and pelting snow. The noise was very loud now, even through the double glazing. It must have been deafening outside. Then, suddenly, a white cone of light burst down through the night and started circling the field in front of our house. 'What is it, Daddy?' Walt asked, scared, clutching my hand now. I could see other lights up there in the sky, red and blue, flashing and blinking around where the white spot began.

'It's a helicopter.' My mouth was dry.

As I said this it revealed itself; coming belly down out of the darkness, the black number '157' painted on its white underside, the windows and floor vibrating, rattling, as it came down into the field just a hundred yards or so from the house, wobbling as it set down on long runners. 'Wow!' Walt said, his terror turning to excitement.

My emotions were already running in the exact opposite direction to Walt's. Because now I could read the gold lettering on the door of the machine, the door that was already opening, two figures jumping down and ducking under the chopping rotors, running towards the house.

I could read the words 'Saskatchewan Police Department'.

And then I was running, sprinting up the half-flight of stairs and into the kitchen, fumbling with the lock that opened the sliding doors out onto the decking, my hands shaking, trying to block out Walt's jabbering stream of enquiries behind me. *The phones are all out and the roads are closed. But – to have flown here in this weather? Oh Jesus.* I was picturing pile-ups, emergency rooms, as I watched the two figures, the policemen, wading through the knee-deep snow towards us, pulling the brims of their hats down, trying to keep them from blowing off in the backdraught from the blades. With a heavy snap I finally unsnicked the lock and slid the door open, a freezing blast of air hitting me in the face. Walt tried to follow me out onto the deck in his T-shirt. 'Walt! Stay in here!'

'But –'

'Fucking STAY, Walt!' For a second I thought he was going to cry. I placed a hand on his shoulder. 'Sorry, son, it's too cold out there. Just wait here a minute. OK?' He turned sulkily back into the kitchen as I stepped out onto the deck, sliding the door shut behind me as I watched the policemen coming up the steps towards me, everything getting quieter as the helicopter powered down, the rotors making a slower shucking sound. I could see the pilot in the cockpit, snapping up switches and pulling toggles. *Oh Jesus Christ, oh Jesus Christ, please let everything be OK, please be OK.* Everything slowed down, like they say it does, and I felt like I was treading through deep ocean as I moved towards the lead figure, a man, older than me, in his fifties, with a silvery moustache, his face wet with snow as he removed his glove and extended a cold hand for me to shake and I knew he was saying my name but I couldn't hear him. I just said, 'Yes?'

'I'm Sergeant Danko, Regina PD. This is Officer Hudson.' I noticed, with faint surprise, that Hudson was a woman.

'It's my wife, Sammy. Isn't it? Something's happened.'

'I'm afraid so.'

Oh Christ, oh Jesus, she should have stayed at the apartment, please be OK, please be OK, please . . .

'Is there somewhere we can talk privately?' Danko asked.

I looked through the glass and saw Walt standing alone in the kitchen, his head bowed a little, watching us shyly through his fringe.

18

DANKO SAT down across the low coffee table from me in the living room, our dinner plates still lying on it. Walt stayed in the kitchen with Hudson. He had taken his hat off, revealing thick silver hair, some of it plastered to his head with sweat. He was explaining about the phone lines being down, twisting his hat in his hands as he spoke, turning it like a steering wheel.

'Please, Sergeant, is she badly hurt?'

'I'm afraid we think she's dead.'

A tidal rush of nausea, a vertiginous *whooshing*, like I had suddenly woken up to find myself teetering on the brink of a chasm, tiny pebbles skittering from under my toes, falling into nothingness. I closed my eyes and covered my face with my hands, trying to take deep breaths as my mind

scrambled around, trying to latch onto something.
I got there after a few seconds.

'You think?' I said.

A mistake. This is all a mistake.

'Well.' Danko swallowed and I saw now how
nervous he was. This scared me more than anything
so far, because this was an old cop. A seasoned guy
who I sensed had surely done this kind of thing
more times than he would have liked, who had sat
in many living rooms and kitchens delivering life-
ending news like this.

'We haven't been able to positively identify the
body yet. A credit card belonging to your wife was
found with the victim but there's, and this won't
be easy for you to hear, sir, there's considerable,
ah, damage to . . .'

All these words, ripping me to pieces. 'Victim?'
I manage to whisper.

'I'm afraid so, yes. It appears your wife was
murdered.'

Now I felt tears and racking sobs trying to
fight their way up, hearing myself saying 'Oh
Sammy, oh no', as my eyes landed on a Lucite-
framed photograph on the coffee table; the three
of us in Hawaii a couple of Christmases ago, on
the beach, Sammy drying Walt with a big beige

towel. Uselessly I remembered that afternoon; a
long wait for appetisers in a restaurant. An
argument about parking. Walt's life as he knew
it – over.

'Mr Miller, I'm afraid we . . .' Danko was
saying.

I knew what he was going to ask me next.

'We need . . .'

'You need me to identify the body,' I said, through
clenched teeth, through my fingers.

He nodded, sadly.

'I . . . I can't. I can't put Walt through that.'

'Officer Hudson can stay here with your son.
She's a trained psychologist and very good with
children. We should be there and back in less than
an hour. Unless you have someone nearby he'd be
more comfortable with?'

'I, have, there . . . there's a neighbour.'

He nodded again. 'Mr Miller, in the circumstances,
it might be better just to tell your son that your
wife's been involved in an accident and that you'll
be back soon.'

I rang Irene from the hall. She answered on the
second ring. The helicopter. 'Sammy's had an accident,' I told her, practising a version of the lie I
was about to tell Walt. 'I need to go into Regina
with the police. To the hospital. I don't want to

take Walt. I'm so sorry, Irene, but do you think you could . . . ?'

'Oh God. Oh dear Lord. Of course, Donnie. Do you, is, is she OK?'

'I think it . . . it's quite bad, Irene.'

For a second I almost believe this version of events. I briefly picture myself walking into a hospital room, seeing Sammy with tubes coming out of her. Bruised and cut but alive. Kissing her tenderly on the forehead, her smiling weakly, woozy on painkillers, as she tells me about the tailgating on the icy highway.

'Oh no, oh God,' Irene said. 'I . . . I'll be right over.'

In the end Walt bought the accident version of events much more easily than I had imagined. He looked worried, but, maybe, more jealous that I was getting to go on the helicopter. 'I'll be back in about an hour,' I told him, zipping up my parka and looking for my gloves as there was a gentle knock at the glass door. Danko opened it and Irene came in nervously, nodding hellos. 'Thanks for coming, Irene.'

'Not at all,' she said. 'I brought a few things, just in case you're longer than you expected.' She set down her bag, a big old Gladstone, Mary Poppins-type thing. 'Are you sure it's OK to fly in this weather, Officer?'

'Yes, ma'am,' Danko said. 'We can get up and around it.'

'OK then,' I said, leaning down and hugging Walt again, feeling sobs trying to fight their way up into my chest. I took a sharp breath in through my nose. 'See you both soon.'

The helicopter went straight up. Ascending almost vertically for thirty, forty feet – with me waving back at Irene and Walt who were standing at the brightly lit kitchen windows – before the pilot dipped the nose and we powered into the wind, veering away from the house, rising in a gradual turn, snow whirling all around us.

Danko and I were in the back, cramped in front of a gun rack: a pair of pump-action shotguns, an assault rifle. As we got higher up, as it got quieter, he leaned in and started to tell me the facts.

Sammy had left the office around eleven thirty for an unscheduled meeting. She may have taken a call on her cellphone that initiated this meeting. Her cellphone had still not been found. Her colleagues assumed she'd headed straight home after lunch somewhere downtown, to beat the storm. Her body was discovered by two city workers on a vacant lot on the eastern outskirts of Regina at six fifteen that evening, her purse and ID nearby.

When had I last seen her? At the party. As she walked away from me, back towards the fireplace and the advertising conversation. Hitching the strap of her gown up.

I let my head drop down, started to cry. Danko looked the other way.

If I had known that would be the last time I would get to talk to her I would have kissed her on the mouth. I would have told her how much I loved her and thanked her for giving us Walt and being such a good mother to him. I'd have told her about all the things I remembered from our years together, all the things we had never spoken of that were burned into my mind forever. Tiny stupid moments.

Sammy giggling and saying 'Oh, *right* . . . .' as I clumsily leaned across the bar-room table to kiss her for the first time.

Sammy laughing when she discovered how scared of spiders I was.

Sammy on the hotel bed, looking up at me, across my stomach, her chin slick as she said, 'Boy, I've had my protein today.'

Sammy crying so hard the first time we argued.

Sammy's guilty expression when I caught her by surprise in a fast-food place downtown, about to bite into a burger.

Sammy lying back after she'd given birth to Walt, woozy from blood loss, pale as a geisha, yet smiling as she watched me holding him.

I remember it all, Sammy. Everything.

19

IT WAS about a week after Banny tried to make
the Professor eat the bit of paper that it happened,
in Miss Gilchrist's English class.

It was the last period of the day and everyone
was tired and listless in the hot, late-spring classroom. Miss Gilchrist had colourful, kind of funny
philosophical posters on her walls: a cartoon child
on a stool, fist on chin, thinking, with a bubble
above his head saying, 'Sometimes I sits and thinks
and sometimes I just sits.' Four cows in different
fields, separated by barbed-wire fencing, each cow
poking its head through the fence to eat the other
cow's grass.

We were doing the poem 'In the Snack Bar'
by Edwin Morgan. I don't know why she suddenly
rounded on Banny that day. Maybe she'd had
enough of his staring out the window, blatantly

not listening, defacing his jotter, or the desk, never paying attention. Maybe it was the near-ceaseless babbling and sniggering with Tommy sitting next to him. Whatever the reason, she interrupted Jackie Shaw's endless monotone reading of the poem ('hiss-of-the-coffee-machine-voices-and-laughter-smell-of-a-cigar-hamburgers-wet-coats-steaming') and said, 'Derek Bannerman?'

Banny looked up, breaking off from whatever he was saying to Tommy. 'Whit?'

'Excuse me?'

A sigh. 'Whit, *Miss?*'

'Why do you think the poet chooses these particular images here?'

A blank stare. Vacant hatred. 'Ah don't know, Miss.'

'Well, I'm asking you to think about it, Derek.'

A long silence. Miss Gilchrist perched on the edge of the desk, her arms folded, poetry book dangling from one hand, as all thirty-odd faces in the class turned towards Banny. Just by asking this question she had broken one of the unspoken rules that surrounded a pupil like Banny, a rule that said, roughly, 'Leave me alone and I will allow you to teach the rest of the class. Fuck with me at your peril.' She had breached etiquette and had to expect a reaction. Banny fidgeted for a second, fingering his tattered, defaced copy of *Seven Modern Poets*, waiting for her to sigh and say, 'Anyone else?' Waiting for hands to go shooting up and things to move on. But she didn't, she stared him down, Banny getting agitated under the fluorescent strip lighting. Finally he shrugged and said, 'Cause he's a fucking bentshot, Miss?'

The class exploded; a fifty–fifty blend of laughter and gasps. Miss Gilchrist let it subside and said, 'Yes. I do sometimes wonder why you think nearly everyone we study in here is gay, Derek.'

There was a further ripple of laughter, at a teacher using the word 'gay', and then, right there in the front row of desks, far away from us at the back, a lone hand went up.

The Professor.

'Yes, Craig?' Gilchrist said.

'Please, Miss, it's called "denial". Derek thinks everyone is gay because he's secretly worried he might be gay himself.'

It is difficult to convey the effect this statement had on the room. A few people laughed – just at the continued repetition of the word 'gay' – but most of us just stared open-mouthed at the Professor before slowly turning to Banny to see what his reaction was going to be, the enormity of the situation slowly dawning: *the Professor just* called *Big Banny a bentshot in front of the whole fucking class.*

Banny was slowly going very, very red. He was getting a roaster, a red neck. A fucking beamer. I felt my own face warming, flushing.

At the party, at his dad's house, the glimpse into the murk of the bedroom. Straightening, buckling up. Banny's stare, fierce. Defiant. Tommy starting to say something that day, starting to say, 'Mind that time?' then tailing off, running off towards those empty ginger bottles. 'Ah've fingered her . . . ah've rode her . . . she's a bike . . . ye don't look at the mantelpiece when yer poking the fire, wee man . . .' In the cold tent, the crackle of the dying fire, the pressure on my groin, his breath hot on my neck, the smell of vodka and lager. Pushing against me, hard, urgent. 'C'mon . . .'

Tommy was the first to speak. He laughed mirthlessly and said, 'You're dead, Docherty.'

'OK, that's enough,' Miss Gilchrist cut in. 'Now, let's get back to the poem. Jackie, where were you?'

The lesson went on, but no one was listening. Everyone was stealing glances at Banny who, incredibly, had still said nothing. He was staring at the back of the Professor's head, a fury glittering in his eyes beyond anything I had ever seen before.

He battered the Professor over by the trees

after final bell. Docherty just went foetal and took it all as Banny flailed and pummelled into him with feet and fists, a tasselled weejun connecting with his mouth, busting his lip open, a fist smacking again and again off Docherty's red, swelling ear, and then a couple of teachers were running over and pulling Banny off. Docherty's parents came into school and saw the headmaster and went mental and Banny got suspended for a week and that was it, over.

But it wasn't. The battering wasn't enough for Banny. Not nearly enough. A poofy wee tool like Craig Docherty? You'd batter someone like that for looking at you the wrong way. What did you do to make restitution for calling you a bender in front of the whole class? No, a kicking wasn't going to cover it. Not even close. We all knew that.

20

I WAS sitting on an orange plastic chair in an office, an anteroom of some kind off the main morgue, down in the basement.

We came down from the rooftop helipad in a freight elevator and then through a series of gently downward-sloping corridors. Hospitals, with their forests of signage – 'Paediatrics', 'Oncology', 'X-Ray' – and their endless bustle. It occurred to me as we came down in the ancient, clanking, brass-gated elevator that the last time I was in Regina General had been nearly nine years ago. When Walt was born. ('Hostibal,' Walt used to say when he was tiny. Like 'bullets' were always 'buttels' to him.)

The pathologist, a Dr Manuel, was sitting next to me, Danko opposite, both of them waiting patiently for an answer to the question Manuel had just asked me. He was balding, bespectacled and tired-looking, not just tired in the sense that he looked like he could use a good night's sleep, he looked tired of all of it, of what we can do to each other. As I guessed you might when your job involved looking at the worst things nature, accidents and man can serve up on a daily basis. I turned the terrible question over in my mind for a long time while I stared at a set of silver kidney-shaped bowls on a table next to Danko, the bowls arranged concentrically, in decreasing sizes, like a cross section of a metallic Russian doll (the useless thought: *How many human organs have been placed in those bowls? Will Sam's . . .*) until finally I answered in a quiet voice.

'She has a . . . a little strawberry birthmark on her, just at the line of the pubic hair.'

Manuel nodded and sat quietly, staring at the floor, and then asked, 'Is there anything else?'

I thought for a moment before turning to look at him. 'Won't that do?' I said.

Manuel held my gaze sadly. The enormity of what he was saying hit me and a fresh wave of horror broke upon me.

'Oh God.' I said. 'Oh Jesus.'

'Mr Miller,' Manual said gently, 'I don't want you to have to view any more of the remains than is strictly necessary. It's your choice of course, but

I really think it would be much better for you to remember your wife as you last saw her.'

Yes, just like you told Walt about Herby.

'I . . . there . . .' I flailed around, trying to remember Sammy's body, ashamed of myself for not being able to recall every inch of her, nausea within me again, my hand covering my face. 'On her right arm, there's a brown birthmark on the inside of the forearm. Like a map of Italy.'

Manuel nodded and stood up. 'If you're ready then.'

The morgue itself: a large room, cold, as it must be, with a bitter chemical smell. Manuel led the way and Danko walked behind me, almost as though they were guarding me, as though I might crack and make a run for it and for a second the thought crossed my mind: sprint out of here, get to the airport, get on a plane, disappear.

But, once you become a parent, these options are removed from the menu. I thought of my son – at home, hopefully sleeping now – and this actually made me calmer. *At the very least you must be stronger than Walt.* There was someone who would be even closer to the vortex of pain than I was. (Sam's parents' too. That call would have to be made soon. They'd have just arrived. I pictured them unpacking in their suite, or maybe already out by the pool or on the beach when the call that would destroy their lives arrived.)

There were three stainless-steel autopsy tables in the middle of the room. On the furthest away one lay a black rubber body bag. Manuel turned to me and said, 'If you'd just wait here, Mr Miller.' He turned back to the table and I heard the *riiiip* of a zipper being pulled along.

This could all still be a mistake.

I allowed the thought I had been quietly nurturing to have a brief final flourish in my mind before Manuel stood aside and I saw he was gently holding a forearm out of the bag, the hand flopping out, the fingers curled inwards, towards the palm.

The coral-pink nail varnish.

I nodded. 'That's Sammy.'

Before I knew what I was doing I reached out and took her hand – it was already cold, the fingers stiff and clutching – and I found myself thinking of the last time I had held her hand on a hospital table, somewhere above us, in this very building: *all your attention focused on Sammy, because you are not good with gore, saying 'Push, baby, push, c'mon, you're doing good' and not looking the other way at all until you heard the crying and the midwife was nudging you and holding out a bloody green towel with a tuft of black hair jutting up from it. There were supposed to be more kids but it didn't seem to happen and then Sam was complaining of stomach pains. After the operation as she wiped away a single tear and smiled, she said, 'Walt's perfect. He's enough.' 'Walt's enough,' you agreed.*

Lost in this, Danko and Manuel respectfully silent, my eyes travelled upwards, across her wrist and onto the faint, coffee-coloured map of Italy. Then I was doubling up, folded in half by an agonising, dry rush of vomit. Because, unable to help myself, I had peered upward, beyond the birthmark, further up Sammy's arm and into the dark space of the body bag. I saw something smooth and white at the top of the arm and I knew it was bone, that the skin had been flayed off her upper arm.

Then I was on my knees, Danko steadying me as I convulsed, Manuel quickly sliding a plastic bucket in front of me as it all came up: a torrent of duck, spinach and rice, all in a stinging, acidic broth of bloody wine, pumping into the bucket, the agonised sound of my vomiting reverberating around the large, cold room.

21

BACK IN the anteroom I carefully sipped the paper cupful of water they'd produced from somewhere, my hands still trembling. After what felt like a long time I spoke quietly. 'I need to call Sammy's parents. They're in Hawaii.'

'We can do that if you'd rather,' Danko said. I looked up, realising that it was just the two of us in here now, and shook my head. Old Sam. The media. This would be huge news. Walt.

'Mr Miller,' Danko began, 'I need to ask, do you and your wife have any enemies?'

'Enemies? I, well, Sammy was a newspaper editor. You piss a few people off sometimes but . . .'

'It's just, the nature of this attack, the severity, it seems almost . . . personal.'

He let it hang for a moment. I looked at him

and said, 'Sergeant, just tell me. If there's anything else I should hear, just tell me.'

'This won't be easy to hear.' He cleared his throat. 'We found needle marks and bruising in the crook of the left elbow, consistent with the recent insertion of an IV drip. There were also ligature marks on both legs and the right arm, suggesting attempts had been made to staunch the bleeding.'

I was just looking at him at this point.

'The blood work confirmed that high levels of saline and sodium thiopental — an anaesthetic — had been administered in the hours before her death.'

'I don't under—'

But I knew. I knew where he was going. But I just kept looking at him, making him say it.

'It seems like someone kept her alive while they tortured her for some time.'

And now real fear kicked in on top of the horror.

I was going to go home and get the loaded gun from my desk drawer and stick it down the front of my pants and get Walt and get on a plane and get the fuck out of here. I was going to call Mike Rawls and tell him to come and get me and Walt and not to leave our side until whoever had done this to Sammy was locked up. Thinking of Walt, of protecting him, refreshed me, shot a jolt of electricity through me.

'I need to call Sammy's parents,' I said, standing up. 'Then I want to go home. Right now.'

22

'ROGER THAT,' the pilot said as Regina unspooled quickly below us; my stomach lurching up into my raw throat as the brilliant intersections and sodium lights of downtown quickly gave way to the sparser blocks of light of the suburbs, then just the acres of white below us, the flatness of Saskatchewan, just the glow of the odd farmhouse. Suddenly, with a bang and the feeling of being smacked hard across the sky, the helicopter was blown hard to the right, reeling sideways, the rotors whining in protest as I was thrown across the small cabin and into Danko. 'Jesus Christ,' I said.

'Hang on back there,' the pilot said, shouting over his shoulder, the instruments glowing green and orange around him, the black night in front of him studded with white tracers of snow. 'This is gonna be pretty rough. Storm's moving around a lot.'

I clung on tight to the strap hanging by my window as the helicopter buffeted around, the pilot trying to climb, to get up above it.

I replayed the short conversation I'd just had with Old Sam. His life had been an idyll before that moment: the two of them lying on loungers, the Pacific sun warm on their faces, the splash of swimmers and the clack and clank of waiters setting down food and drink, the smell of suntan lotion and grilling seafood.

Then the manager — whom I'd personally insisted find Mr Sam Myers and take him some-where private to receive the call — leading him off to an office, or to their suite, and then Old Sam gruffly saying 'Yeah?', probably convinced that this was some business nonsense that could have been delayed or delegated. (Though he is good with neither.) Then I was telling him what had happened, omitting the very worst of it, but it still sounding mad and fantastical and just unreal as it came out of my mouth. Silence at first and then a sound I had never heard before — Sam Myers crying.

'Hang on!' The pilot shouted. We were dropping now, struggling to hold our line against the snow, which seemed to be coming in horizontally, and I could see our house in front of and below us, just visible through the blizzard, the lights in the wall of windows along the kitchen blazing. Another bang and the helicopter almost swung around 180 degrees. 'Fuck!' the pilot said, the panic in his voice scaring me more than anything so far. He was struggling with the joystick, trying to keep us level, to keep the nose pointed into the gale. I could see Irene at the window, silhouetted, watching, as we dropped the last thirty, twenty feet, and then a soft crumping from under us as the helicopter came down into the snow, which was much deeper than when we'd left, sinking down up to its belly, up to the doors. The three of us – Danko, the pilot and me – all exhaled as one.

'Nicely done, Matt,' Danko said, leaning over and putting a hand on the guy's shoulder. He was flipping switches, killing the engine, the rotors already starting to power down above us.

'I'm gonna stay here and talk to control,' the pilot said. I saw now in the instrument glow that his face was bathed in sweat. 'I don't know if we'll get back through that again tonight.'

Irene held the sliding door to the kitchen open for us, looking at me with concern, apprehension, as we came in. The kitchen was warm and filled with cooking smells.

'I put a lasagne from the freezer in the oven,' Irene said. 'I didn't know if you'd be —'

'Is Walt sleeping?' I asked.

'I doubt it. He only went down ha—'

'Sammy's dead, Irene.'

Her hands flew to her face, covering her mouth as though she might scream. 'She was murdered.' She did scream then, stifling it with her hands. Danko and Hudson stood behind me, hats off, looking at their boots as Irene came towards me, crying, shaking her head, and we embraced, her big, red, perfumed hair tickling my nose. I was conscious of the breadth of her shoulders.

'Oh God, oh dear God, Donnie,' she sobbed into my neck. 'How? Why would —' She slumped down into a chair, crying into a tea towel. I crossed the room to the cupboard where we kept the liquor and took out a bottle of brandy and some glasses.

'What happened?' Irene asked, breathing hard, dabbing at her eyes with the towel.

'I'm going to go and talk to Walt. Get it over with.' I was already pouring myself a huge slug of Rémy Martin. 'Maybe Sergeant Danko can . . .'

Danko nodded as, just then, his radio crackled into life. 'Sorry,' he said, holding up a finger, then, into the radio, 'Go ahead.'

'Yeah, she's moved right around between us and Regina.' Matt, the pilot, crackly and metallic. 'We don't have enough fuel to fly far enough around. No way out of here tonight, I'm afraid.'

'Roger that,' Danko said.

'I'm gonna run some checks. Get a little rest.'

'Sorry,' Danko said, turning the radio back down. 'Looks like we might have to impose on you for the night, Mr Miller.'

'Donnie's fine. And don't worry, we've plenty of room.' I drained my glass and poured another. 'OK.'

As I headed out of the kitchen, down the hallway towards Walt's room, I could hear Danko talking to Irene, starting to tell her about Sammy leaving the office unexpectedly that morning. I looked out of the window, towards the pool house, and thought of Herby. Thought of something out there in the storm, stalking us. Stalking what was left of my family. I glanced down the long hallway that ran off to my right, leading to my office, and remembered the gun. I'd get it in a minute, after I'd talked to Walt. I gulped down the brandy, set the glass on the window ledge, and walked on down the hall.

Walt was sitting up in bed with his new phone. He put it down guiltily as I entered. 'I was just —' he began.

'It's OK,' I said, sitting down on the edge of his bed, aware as I did so that I was suddenly slightly drunk, but that the drink was coming nowhere close to taking the edge off my nerves. My vision was swimming. The only light in the room came from the powder-blue night light, plugged into the wall socket by his bed. Walt's fear of the dark. *Will he ever get over that now?* There were clothes and toys strewn all over the room; cars and guns and swords and helmets, totems Walt would be outgrowing soon, teenage years now beginning somewhere around ten or eleven. There, on his bedside table, was a plate with crumbs and a mug with a film of hot chocolate in the bottom. Sammy must have brought it to him the morning before, before she left for work. Would it have been the last motherly duty she performed for the boy? Did she kiss him as she placed it there? Chastise him for still being in bed? These thoughts piled in too quickly, on top of each other, and I found that I had to put my face in my hands and breathe deeply, and before I knew it, I was crying and reaching for Walt's hand.

'Daddy,' Walt said. 'What's wrong? Is it . . .'

'Mummy had an accident,' I said. 'She . . . she's dead, son.'

With those words I ended Walt's childhood.

He started blinking rapidly, a nervous tick he
has. His eyes were darting around the room,
refusing to meet mine, panic setting in. 'Where is
she? When will she come home?'

'She's at the hospital. She isn't coming home,
Walt.'

I'm really crying now, scaring him even more.

'No!' Walt says fiercely. *I want to see Mommy!*

I flash on that white nub of bone.

'Oh, son. You can't . . .'

'NO!'

I pull Walt to me as his tears begin, hot against
my neck.

We held each other, crying softly for a long time,
until I became aware of a gentle knocking at the
door. 'Come in,' I said thickly and Officer Hudson
came in holding a glass of chocolate milk, milk I
knew was laced with Valium. 'Hi, Walt,' she said.
'I brought you a drink.'

She sat down next to Walt on the bed. 'Ow!'
She winced as she sat down and adjusted her
black police-issue waistcoat. 'What's wrong?' Walt
sniffed.

'Look,' Hudson said. She unzipped the waistcoat
and showed Walt a metal panel hidden in the
lining.

'What's that?' Walt asked.

'It stops bullets. Like Superman.'

Walt knocked his fist against the metal, fascin-
ated.

'Knock knock,' Hudson said.

23

'SHE'S VERY good,' Danko said softly, as I poured us both another brandy. 'Hudson? One of the best I've worked with at this sort of thing.' I nodded, looking at the snow sheeting sideways past the windows, the wind audible even through the thick glass. The helicopter was half buried now. Irene moved around in the background, gathering cutlery and plates. It was nearly ten o'clock. 'Donnie,' Danko said after a moment, 'if you want to be on your own . . .'

'No, it's OK. I just . . .' I was hollow, all adrenalin burned off. Talking to Walt had taken about everything I had in me.

'Did you speak to Sammy's parents?' Irene asked quietly.

'They're trying to get on the last flight out of Hawaii tonight. Gets into LA around six tomorrow morning. They probably won't be here until tomorrow night.' Irene nodded. I pictured Sammy's parents on the flight, lost in grief in first class.

The door opened and Hudson came in. 'He's asleep.'

'Thank you,' I said. 'Did . . . did he say anything?'

'Not much. He wanted to see my gun. He was exhausted.'

Silence. The wind. The hum of the oven.

'Sorry,' Hudson said. 'Is there somewhere I could get some rest? Been at it since five this morning.'

'Sure,' I said getting up. 'I'll –'

'You sit down, Donnie,' Irene said, passing behind my chair, touching my shoulder. 'I'll show Officer Hudson one of the guest rooms. I put the pilot, Mr –'

'Matt,' Danko said.

'I put Matt in the room down the end.'

'Thanks, Irene.'

'Goodnight,' Hudson said.

'Please,' I said, turning back to Danko, 'if you want to turn in too, go right ahead.'

'I'll stay up and finish this, if that's OK?' He raised his brandy tumbler. 'Maybe have some of that lasagne.'

'Sure.' I was glad. I wanted conversation,

distraction. Anything to keep me from picturing what I knew I was going to be picturing as soon as I was alone. *Tortured her.* I realised I was going to be picturing that every day for the rest of my life. Walt too, once he was old enough to understand everything that happened. To google his mother's name and read the newspaper reports online. I shook my head, shaking those thoughts away, and sipped my drink. Danko looked around the huge kitchen and said, 'Very nice place you have here, Donnie.'

The utter unreality of the situation – sitting in our kitchen, drinking brandy with the policeman who had come to tell me that my wife was dead – suddenly hit me and a short bark of laughter escaped me. 'Christ. Sorry,' I said, 'it's just so . . .'

'Don't be,' Danko said. 'Funnily enough, it's a fairly common reaction.'

'Have you done a lot of this kind of thing?'

'More than I'd have liked to.' He shook his head, repeated it. 'More than I'd have liked to.'

'It must be hard on you guys too.'

'Well, you get some folk just can't do it. I used to work with a fella, Ellison, was it?' He scratched his silvery stubble, thinking. 'Yeah, Joe Ellison. He –' Danko stopped and looked up at me. 'Sorry, you sure you want to hear about this stuff?'

I nodded and reached for the bottle.

'Well, we had to go and tell this couple their daughter had been killed. RTA, north of here, near Moosejaw. We were partners, but we hadn't been working together long. This was some years back, you understand. Anyway, I'd done the last one we had, talked to the family? So it was his turn and he didn't want to do it. "Come on, Joe," I said. "Fair's fair. I did the last one." So, we got in there, and as soon as folk see you unexpectedly they're thinking the worst of course, and he says, "I'm afraid we have some bad news concerning your daughter." And this woman, straight away, she just says, "She's dead!" And Joe says, "You're right!" and he bursts out laughing.' I laughed. 'Yeah. He just couldn't handle . . . the intensity of the whole thing. Boy, we got torn to pieces by the Captain on that.' Danko shook his head as I topped us up.

The door opened and Irene came back in, humming with womanly efficiency, wearing oven gloves as she headed for the stove.

'I guess it's just too much for some people to handle,' Danko said. 'Laughing like that? Just a kink in the old fight or flight mechanism.' He sipped his drink and spoke over his shoulder to Irene. 'Boy that smells good, ma'am.' Irene came over and stood behind him, smiling, still wearing the oven mitts. 'I guess that brandy's sharpened my appetite up. I —'

There was a soft, rapid popping noise — three 'pops' in quick succession — and Danko suddenly jerked bolt upright in his chair, as though an electrical current had been shot through him, his face screwed up in agony, his feet kicking out, hitting the table, sending his glass skittering across it. I jumped back, terrified, thinking he was having a stroke, or a heart attack. He sat bolt upright, clutching the edge of the table, frozen for a second, his eyeballs fluttering up in their sockets.

Blood began to pour from the corner of his mouth.

He smashed face first down onto the wooden table. The back of his head was a bloody mess.

Standing directly behind him; Irene.

Her oven-gloved right arm was extended to exactly where the back of Danko's head had been a moment ago and the tip of the glove was charred and smoking, with a ragged hole in it. I was stumbling backwards, shaking, trying to speak, trying for a handhold on something — the chair back, the counter — as Irene shook her hand from side to side, allowing the glove to fall off.

She was holding a small automatic pistol. Smoke wreathed from its muzzle.

She was smiling, a broad awful grin.

The pool of blood spreading out from Danko's head was already dripping onto the floor. His leg was twitching.

The smell of cordite filled the kitchen.

'Hello, William,' Irene said.

Her Georgia accent was changing, becoming something else.

24

SHE CAME around behind me, this woman that I knew now was not Irene Kramer from Georgia, and I could feel the hot muzzle of the gun very close to my neck. I was very sober now, nausea rising in me with the terror. Danko's body twitched again and I jumped. 'Easy, William,' she said. 'Put your hands behind your back, through the slats of . . . that's it.'

'Why are you calling me that? What's —'

Screeching pain as she smacked me on the forehead with the butt of the gun. 'Don't lie to me again.' I could feel cold metal slipping around my wrists and every cell in my body recoiled, screaming, *Do not let this woman handcuff you to this chair.* I tensed, ready to spring forward, and, instantly, the smoking muzzle was in my neck, just under my ear, burning me. 'Don't,' she said, and I heard the 'snick' of the cuffs ratcheting home.

I was crying, my head hung, saying 'Please' as she stepped in front of me and said, 'Look at me.'

I looked up, knowing now that it was her. Knowing it, but not really believing it. I could make no connection with the elderly red-headed woman standing above me and the young blonde I had last seen in a grainy online file photo, or the last time I had seen her in the flesh, in court, nearly thirty years ago. A lifetime. 'What's my name?' she said. The Georgia accent was completely gone now, replaced by a west coast of Scotland brogue, a gentler, more refined version of my own. *The theatre group. Amateur dramatics.*

'Mrs Docherty,' I said, through sobs. 'Gill Docherty.'

'Good boy, William. That's better.'

'You killed Sammy. Our dog . . .'

'Plenty of time to discuss all that. We've got all night. You'll never know how much planning went into all this. My life's work, actually.' She was rooting in her bag now, bringing something out, something shining in her hand. A silver disc. 'I ran this off earlier,' she said as she crossed towards the TV and slipped the disc into its side.

She pressed 'PLAY' — a jarring burst of static and then a picture appeared.

Sammy.

Naked, lashed to a chair with silver electrical tape. Her face was slick with blood and sweat and she was crying and screaming noiselessly. Then Gill Docherty was thumbing the remote and the green bars were going across the bottom of the screen as the volume went up and then Sammy's screams were filling the kitchen. She was saying *'Oh please, oh God, oh God, oh Jesus, oh please stop!'* and I could see, just on the edge of the shot, the top of Irene's head, shaking, her elbow moving in and out in a sawing motion.

I started screaming as hard as I could, drowning the TV out as I shut my eyes and shook violently. Suddenly I felt her arms around my neck, gripping me tightly, the cashmere of her sweater against the side of my face; I could smell her perfume. 'Listen to me, William,' she said, close to my ear, her voice terrifyingly calm. 'Open your eyes. I want you to watch this video.' I felt something very sharp beneath my eye and opened them, seeing the point of a chisel. 'If you close your eyes again I'll cut your eyelids off. Do you understand?' I nodded.

The tears in my eyes made it possible for me to look at the screen but to keep it blurred, unfocused. I could do nothing with my ears. *'JESUSPLEASESTOPNOOHJESUSCHRIST!'* Sammy's pleas were endless, a torrent, until suddenly it went quiet and I blinked, seeing that, on the screen, Sammy's head had flopped forward and she had either died or passed out.

I could see now that she was surrounded by tall, silver stands with milky plastic bags attached to the tops, tubes running down. *Saline and sodium thiopental. Someone kept her alive while . . .*

'You know it's going to be much worse for you, don't you?' She took a cloth and a brown bottle from her bag and smiled at me.

'I WAS JUST A KID!'

'And he punishes the children, and their children,' she said, pouring stuff into the cloth, stepping towards me, 'for the sins of the parents, to the third or fourth generation.' She stuffed the cloth into my face, over my mouth and nose, the intense smell of the ether hitting me, causing nausea and headspin, blackness pouring in as I heard her saying, 'Exodus 34 . . .'

And then I couldn't hear anything.

25

I CAME round with a sharp, throbbing pain in the middle of my forehead. As I opened my eyes I felt the blood caked on my cheek crack and split. I was breathing through my nose and could feel ragged duct tape sealing my mouth. There were wooden stairs leading up in the corner, next to a big gas boiler.

A basement.

I was tied to an old, heavy wooden chair, arms lashed to the arms, legs to the legs. The only light in the room came from an old anglepoise lamp over on a workbench. Directly in front of me was a wooden butcher's block table. Turning my head left, producing another jolt of pain, I could see a small window at shoulder height, probably level with the ground outside. As my eyes adjusted to the darkness I noticed that old mattresses and egg-box cartons had been crudely fixed to all the walls and with tumbling blood I realised why.

Soundproofing.

I started to panic and began pulling and tugging at my bonds when I heard a soft moan. I looked down. Walt was stretched out on the concrete floor beside me. He was hog-tied; his hands and feet lashed together behind his back, a silver strip of gaffer tape covering his mouth. He woke up too, with a jolt, like someone coming round from a terrible dream. He looked around the room, blinking, his chin just off the cement floor and then he looked up and saw me. Walt's eyes widened – I guessed at the amount of blood on my face, from the cut where she smacked me with the gun. We looked at each other, me trying to convey sorrow, apology, reassurance, Christ knows what, with just my eyes. I started frantically tugging my forearms this way and that, looking for some purchase, some give. Nothing. Not an inch. I started rocking the chair from side to side, trying to tip it over, perhaps smash it. The wooden legs scraped and banged on the cement.

Almost immediately, directly above us, I heard footsteps clacking across wooden floorboards.

Breathing hard, sweating, the sweat loosening the

dried blood on my face, I looked over towards the stairs and saw something on the workbench I hadn't noticed before, something I hadn't seen since Walt was tiny: a baby monitor, green-and-white plastic with a steady red LED light indicating that it was on. Then a door creaked open above us, a bar of widening light spilled across the stairs and heavy boots started clumping down.

'Look who's up!'

Mrs Gill Docherty was wearing jeans and a baggy cream sweater. She would have looked like any casually dressed elderly lady were it not for the streak of blood across the sweater and the butcher's knife she was holding.

She put the knife down on the table and picked up Walt, hefted him into a chair, ignoring his wriggling and his muffled 'mmmmffs' and 'uhnnnns' as she started to lash him to it, humming a little tune to herself, looking very much like a mechanic wrestling with a piece of machinery. I was shouting into my gag now, making terrible, beseeching noises. Once she'd tied Walt in place she crossed over to me. I felt a chunk of my lip come off as she tore the gag from my mouth.

'Please, please let him go. I'm begging you. Ire—'

She raised an eyebrow.

'Mrs Docherty, please –'

'We're all grown up now, William. You can call me Gill.'

'Please. It's Walt. You know him. You don't want to hurt him.'

She ignored me and perched easily on the butcher's block table. 'First, it's time to tell your son who you really are.'

Walt looked at me, his nostrils flaring rapidly, shallow, fast terrified breathing.

'I . . . oh Christ. It was so long ago.'

A zinging sound as she picked up the knife, scraping the blade along the wooden table, and brought it up to Walt's cheek, pulling his head back by the hair, Walt screaming uselessly into his gag. 'Please,' she said.

'William. My name is William Anderson.' I said the name aloud for the first time in twenty-nine years, trying very hard not to cry as I said, 'Please don't hurt him.'

'Now, I'd like you to tell Walt what you did.'

'I wasn't the worst one,' I said, feeling how useless it was as I said it.

'But you're the one I found.'

'I was just . . . just a wee boy . . .' I was crying now and Walt started to cry too. She let him go and moved over towards the table. She reached into her bag and began taking things out. 'How did you find me?' I asked.

'All in good time.'

She started to place things on the table in front of us.

A hacksaw.

A silver scalpel.

A huge hunting knife, with brutal serrated teeth.

A car battery.

A chisel.

I went mad: shouting and screaming and crying and violently rocking the chair from side to side.

'Save your strength, William.'

'People will be here soon. The police. Sammy's parents.'

'Not till the morning. We've got all night. All night for a lovely trip down memory lane. Come on now. Tell your son all about it.'

I hung my head, sobbing. 'I can't remember.' I heard her sigh, pick up the knife and step towards Walt again.

I started talking.

26

A SATURDAY morning, sunny and clear. The first week of May 1982. We were down at the river, up near the railway bridge, at the bend that led out towards the sea. We were sitting on the concrete wall by the weir, our legs dangling over the side above the brown, frothy water, throwing stones at an empty Coke can we'd thrown in, seeing who could sink it first. We were talking about the Pope's visit to Scotland the following month.

'If that dirty Fenian bastard comes doon here,' Banny said, 'he'll get his fucken baws booted.'

Tommy laughed. 'Aye, too right. Imagine it, man. Jist runnin' oot and bootin the cunt in the chanks?'

We all laughed.

'UDA, all the way,' Banny said, spitting into the river. 'Fuck the Pope and the IRA,' we chorused.

JOHN NIVEN

Across the river, on the opposite bank, an old guy appeared, walking a dog, a Border collie.

'HO! MISTER!' I shouted. 'ARE YOU RIDING THAT FUCKING DUG!' The guy shook his head and walked on. Banny and Tommy pissed themselves. 'You're aff yer heed so ye are, Wullie,' Tommy said.

Banny threw his last stone hard and smacked it right into the Coke can, with a 'plop' and 'ting' combined. 'See that! Ya fucken dancer!' The red-and-white aluminium bobbled, glugged and sank.

Banny stood up, wiping chalky dust off his Sta-Prest, his Harrington. 'Fuck it, man. This is boring as fuck.' He looked along the empty stretch of riverbank. 'C'mon, we'll go doon the puggies.' The puggies; Defender, Galaxian, Asteroids, Scramble.

'Aye, whit wi?' Tommy asked. 'Ah'm skint.'

Banny shrugged. 'We'll nick some wee fanny's credits.' He'd done this before. Just shoved a kid off the machine when they still had credits remaining, telling the kid he'd put the money in while they were playing. What was some wee fanny going to do to Banny?

'Aye, aw right.' Tommy stood up too. 'It'll be better than this pish.'

Tommy and Banny were standing over me, their

shadows blocking out the sun, when it happened. I heard footsteps, the sound of someone approaching, and then Tommy was saying, 'No way, man. No fucking way.' I could hear the grin in his voice as he said it and then I was getting to my feet and following their gaze.

There he was, coming round the corner of the poured-concrete weir house, a fishing rod in one hand and a small trout dangling from the other. Craig Docherty.

The fucking Professor.

Alone. In the wild.

He saw us and jerked back, like he was thinking about turning and running for it, but Banny was already walking towards him and Docherty froze. Just stood there.

'Aw right, Professor?' Banny said, casually, almost pleasantly. Docherty glanced up and down the riverbank, looking, praying, for an adult to appear. Nothing – just the dog guy, hundreds of yards away on the other side now.

'Whit ye got there?' Tommy said. We were all around him now.

'Trout,' Docherty said quietly. He'd looped a piece of nylon fishing line through the fish's gills and was carrying it by that. He looked utterly miserable, the enormity of the situation dawning on him. The kickings he got at school were, by necessity, brief and hurried. Swiftly terminated by teachers. There was never the opportunity for a kicking outside school because Craig Docherty didn't go anywhere we went. He didn't hang around the puggies, or the chippie. He didn't go to parties. Or discos at the community centre. Now and then you'd see him in the supermarket with his mum.

'Gies it,' Banny said, reaching for the little fish.

Docherty moved it away, behind his leg.

'Fucking gies it,' Banny said, pushing Docherty, snatching it. 'Gads o' fuck!' Banny said, his face screwed up in disgust as he examined the trout. 'Slimy as fuck.' It was brown, about eight inches long, with blood-red mottling standing out on the dark back, the milky-silver underbelly brilliant in the sunshine. 'Whit ye gaunny dae wi it?' Banny asked.

'Take it home,' Docherty said.

Banny tossed the trout into the river, a flicker of white as it sank, floating just below the surface. 'No any more,' Banny said as Docherty watched sadly. He turned away, head down, eyes averted, and went to walk off. 'Hey!' Banny said, catching him by the shoulder. 'Where ye gauin?'

'Aye, we're fucking talking tae ye!' Tommy said.

'Here, ah fancy a bit of fishing maself,' Banny said, grabbing for Docherty's rod.

Docherty pulled the rod tight into his side, the end resting on the ground, like a soldier performing a rifle drill, and shook his head fiercely. Banny pulled, moving in, towering over Docherty, a foot taller.

'Gie him it!' Tommy said, shoving Docherty, who was turning away, trying to shield the rod with his body. Banny grabbed it with both hands and slammed his hips into Docherty, body-checking him hard, sending him flying across the poured concrete, his glasses flying off, the rod in Banny's hands now.

Docherty lay there, looking up at us, breathing hard, his face strange and blank without his glasses. There were tears in his eyes but his jaw was set and his fists were balled. 'Give it back,' he said.

'Nae bother,' Banny said. He snapped the rod cleanly in half over his knee and threw the pieces in Docherty's face. 'There ye go.' Tommy laughed. Then something happened no one was expecting.

Docherty went for Banny.

Instantly, you could tell he'd never been in a fight in his life: head down, fists flailing wildly. Banny, an eight-year veteran of playground battles and street fights, just stepped back and let Docherty reach him, taking a couple of weak, useless punches on the arms before he grabbed Docherty's hair and started slowly pulling his head towards the ground.

'Iya! Iya!' Docherty squealed.

Banny kicked Docherty hard in the face, one, two, three times, then let him go. Docherty staggered back and fell down, blood pouring from his nose and mouth, but trying to get back up, trying to stand on trembling legs.

'C'MON THEN!' Banny screamed.

It became like a dream, like a nightmare, like a video, like one of the horror videos watched on those endless afternoons off school, the curtains closed in the living room of the small council house, the only light coming from the fizzing television. Things happened quickly, fast-forward, and yet seemed to take all the time in the world. Freeze-frame. Slow motion. Banny whipping Docherty with the rod, shouting things I couldn't hear. Tommy, his jaw set terribly as his foot lashed back and forth, real blood on the ox-blood Doc Martens. Above us the sky was cloudless, smiling on the crime, the riverbank empty for miles in both directions. The bushes and the poured-concrete weir house bearing silent witness. Docherty's trousers were pulled off, then his pants, his trembling, bloodied hand as he tried to stop this, tried to hold onto this last shred of dignity ('no, no, no, please, no . . .'), and then the bronze rod was arcing against the blue again, the sun kissing the length of the graphite as it whistled through the air, a filament of silver line trailing behind it. The red welts appearing on his thighs, his buttocks, the blood. More blood. His face – the face I still see every night as I reach for sleep – caked in dirt and tears, a pebble stuck to his cheek, looking at me, begging. Tommy sitting on his back, Banny on his legs, moving the broken end of the rod towards . . .

His scream.

This had all gone far enough, too far, much, much too far. But there was further to go, distance yet to run, as Tommy jumped on his head now, laughing, stumbling, falling over. Then Banny was leaping off the low wall above Docherty. Banny was caught against the sun – his black silhouette framed, arms extended, feet coming down, like at the pool ('No Dive-Bombing'), like an awful bird of prey, falling, falling, his feet the talons, coming straight down at Docherty's skull, Docherty sobbing, trying to crawl, the glittering rod quivering in time with his sobs. Banny's face, lit with terrible glee. The impact . . .

Banny getting up and walking away, straightening his Harrington, brushing chalky dust off, flicking his hair out of his face.

Back into real time and the silence, broken by a gull, crying as it streaked low over the river, white on grey, moving fast in the corner of my eye. Tommy was the first to speak.

'Docherty? Get up, ya cunt.'

They'd told us something, in Physics, about the velocity of falling objects, something to do with mass times gravity or something, about unstoppable forces and immovable objects, but the only person here who would have been listening, who could have told you what the equation was, wasn't listening any more. He wouldn't be listening to anything ever again.

A single rivulet from his ear – black and thick as treacle. His mouth and eyes – both open, the mouth caught as though it was forming the end of the word 'no', the eyes just staring up, staring dumbstruck at the bland, vacant sky.

It was Banny who took charge.

Nobody saw anything.

It was our word against any cunt's.

He told us to get stones and boulders and put them in Docherty's pockets.

We rolled him to the edge of the weir and

pushed him into the water. I tried not to look at him. He floated away, face down, just below the surface, the green parka ballooning up out of the water slightly.

The rest of the weekend was fear and keeping quiet and staying out of the way. I remember feeling sick all that weekend, avoiding my parents, spending most of it in my room, my mum having to call me out for meals. The nauseating fear as we ate, as always, on our laps with the telly on, me pushing the mince and tatties and beans around my plate, unable to look as my dad mashed his into a pink/grey pulp. He changed channels for *Game for a Laugh* after the football results and we watched a couple of minutes of the news, me wondering if this would be it. But no – just a news item about the Pope's visit, about proposed redundancies at a steelworks near Motherwell. The weather. The crack and hiss as my dad opened another can of lager. My mum asking if I was feeling OK? 'Bit sick.' I told her I'd drunk too much ginger.

First thing Monday it was on the news, on the telly, about the missing boy, Craig Docherty aged thirteen from Ardgirvan, Ayrshire. Last seen fishing Saturday morning on the River Irvine near the railway bridge. Docherty's mum and dad, appealing for anyone with information. It was the talk of the school. Rumours about paedos and stuff.

It was in the papers on Tuesday, his face on the cover of the *Daily Record*, his school photo: Docherty smiling in white shirt, school tie and blazer.

The next day the old dog-walker guy came forward with a description of 'three youths' seen at the weir that Saturday morning. They were 'loud and abusive'.

They found the body on Thursday morning. The current had carried it nearly a mile, to within sight of the estuary where the river emptied into the Irish Sea. It had drifted into a bank and become wedged beneath the roots of a tree. A golfer at Bankside, looking for his ball down behind the sixth green had spotted what he thought was just 'a green coat' floating in the water. Given what police described as the 'horrific' nature of his injuries it was now a murder hunt. Police appealed for the three boys seen near the weir to come forward. That night, we later found out, Tommy asked his big sister, 'See if ye didnae mean to kill somebody but they died could ye still go to the jail?' She told her mum and dad. Tommy didn't come into school on Friday morning.

They came for me and Banny during second

period. Chemistry. I remember we were all gathered round a Bunsen burner, wearing the daft
glasses, the knock at the door, Mr Staples looking
up from whatever he was demonstrating as Mr
McMahon, the headmaster entered, looking
shocked. The black, looming figures of the two
policemen behind him and everything seeming to
go into slow motion as they came towards us.
Banny acting indignant, saying 'Whit?' and 'No me'
and Mr McMahon taking me gently by the elbow
and leading me towards the police. The stunned
silence in the class.

I can't really remember the hours and days after
that very clearly, but I know it didn't take long to
break us down. They interviewed Banny and me
separately and we were contradicting each other
within minutes, the whole thing coming apart,
falling down around us. The cell. How hard and
cold the tiled bench was. The toilet in the corner.
The disbelief on my parents' faces. Detectives and
psychologists from Glasgow. Edinburgh even. Being
asked about my home life, about sex, about fighting.
About the incident in Miss Gilchrist's English class
weeks ago. (They'd interviewed everyone in the
class.) The woman who just sat in the corner and
watched me and wrote things down. Glimpsing
Tommy, crying, through the open door of another

interview room. The policemen mainly polite to us, except one older, harder man, with a thick black moustache, who I later learned had seen the body, whispering, hissing, to me as he took me back to the cell after more questioning. 'Yese are cruel, vicious wee bastards. Ah hope they throw away the fucking key.'

By the following week I was 'Boy C'.

27

THE TRIAL in Glasgow, where I last saw her, during the winter of 1982.

It took months for the case to come to court, for profiles to be prepared by psychologists and social workers, for the Procurator Fiscal's office to prepare the prosecution. We were all held in different young offenders institutes: Banny near Edinburgh, Tommy further north, outside Aberdeen, and me closest to home, in Glasgow.

And all the while the Scottish press bayed for our blood. 'Hang them.' 'Pure evil.' The papers dwelt at length on Craig Docherty's stable, loving home. His exceptional academic promise. Our lives were described as 'chaotic' and 'broken'. My parents came to visit two or three times that summer. My mother would sit crying and saying 'Why? Why?' My father – silent, eyeing me coldly until, the last time he came, he stood up after five minutes and said, 'You're no son of mine.' They had to be rehoused twice. The windows kept getting put in, things painted on the walls. ('MURDERER'. 'BASTERDS'.) People spat at them in the street, until, finally, my mum wrote that letter. They didn't come to the trial and I never heard from them again.

I came off best in the reports. I was a 'timid, easily led boy', who had 'the capacity for remorse' and who showed 'some academic promise' and 'potential for rehabilitation'.

Tommy had a 'limited capacity' to understand the consequences of his actions and there was 'very little to suggest' this would ever be improved upon. His IQ was determined at 72, 'borderline feeble minded'.

They went to town on Banny. 'A vicious, malevolent personality' with 'an enormous capacity for cruelty'. They found evidence of sexual abuse. He had great difficulty expressing any 'empathy or remorse' over what had happened. Banny tried longer than any of us to deny killing Craig. He blamed me. Tommy, who my lawyer said was 'intimidated' by Banny, blamed me too. When Banny finally confessed to 'some part' in the murder it was in what the prosecutor characterised as 'a blatant attempt to mitigate sentencing'. In court Tommy and I looked at our feet. Banny stared straight ahead, sullen and defiant. The judge characterised his attitude as 'irritation. As though it were inconvenient that a minor misdeed should keep troubling him.'

I remembered her from the trial. Blonde, full lips. She seemed very old to me then of course, although she couldn't have been more than thirty-four or thirty-five. She watched everything intently, taking notes on an A4 pad, looking from us to the judge, to whichever lawyer was talking. She didn't cry, but her hand would sometimes cover her face when certain details were read out. ('Rectal tearing, dozens of gashes, massive cranial trauma, decomposition of the body after five days in the water.')

We were over twelve, the age of criminal responsibility in Scotland at that time, so we were effectively tried as adults. Banny was convicted of first-degree murder and sentenced to life, defined as being a minimum of fifteen years. Tommy and I were found guilty of second-degree murder and given seven years each, prompting an outcry in the press about soft sentencing. At the Home Secretary's insistence we were mandated to serve the full terms of our sentences with no possibility of parole, meaning we would remain in young offenders institutions until we were eighteen before being transferred to adult prisons to serve the remainder of our time. Then we were to be released into probationary care with new identities.

We were all moved around a lot in our first few years, for our own safety. I stayed in three different institutions across central Scotland in the first two years. Every time I was transferred there would be screaming mobs outside the van, Mr Cardew, holding my hand sometimes, a blanket over my head, the flashbulbs of the press going off.

Tommy never made it. He was stabbed and killed in a borstal fight when he was seventeen.

Banny's sentence was extended by three years due to repeated incidents of violence. He was finally released on parole in 2000, when he was thirty-two. He almost immediately reoffended, raping a fourteen-year-old girl. He is still in prison today.

I was luckier: Mr Cardew, *Of Mice and Men*, *The Long and the Short and the Tall* (the way the dying boy said 'mother', always strangely affecting to me). Ted Hughes. 'The Jaguar'. ('Over the cage floor, the horizons come.' Mr Cardew explaining its resonance to my situation.) Then Shakespeare and me crying and shaking in his arms, smelling the nicotine on his jacket. We had to stop. Orwell and Larkin. I learned to play chess, Mr Cardew gradually becoming Paul over hours at the board while I became Donald Miller. By the time I was eighteen the thirteen-year-old William Anderson already felt remote and half remembered, like a distant relative, a second cousin who shared a vague trace element in the blood, an echo in the bone structure, but who I didn't really know, whose history I did not share and was not responsible for. (Perhaps true to a degree for all teenagers.) I was given a backstory: my parents died when I was very young and I was brought up by an elderly uncle who died when I was eighteen, the uncle finally fusing in my mind with Mr Cardew.

I took what we had done, what I had done, sealed it up in a box, and dropped into the depths of my being.

I was released in 1989 and matriculated at Lampeter University in Wales that October as Donald Angus Miller. A mature student at one of the smallest, most remote universities in the UK.

Biology helped me. A twenty-year-old is almost unrecognisable from his thirteen-year-old self, the age at which all available photographs of me were last taken. As an undergraduate I sported a thick, unfashionable growth of beard. The government paid me a living allowance and kept watch at a distance. The gentrification of the soul that had begun in prison with books was intensified at university with life. I met English people for the first time, people we would have called 'posh' or 'up themselves', and I marvelled at their ease in the world, at the way they laughed as they casually held up a hand to bring a waiter to the table. I didn't drink wine, didn't see a bottle of wine, until I was twenty years old, at an arts faculty 'cheese and wine' at Lampeter. Some kind of thick, rusty Bulgarian red, served in plastic cups. The token plates of Jarlsberg and Brie curling untouched on the side, under the strip lighting of the lecture theatre.

There were some upper-middle-class children at Lampeter, the sons and daughters of wealthy London or Home Counties families whom even the best public schools had failed to springboard into Oxbridge, Bristol or St Andrews. I went to my first dinner party later the same year, hosted by two girls (Hilary and Ally?) in their flat off-campus, the dining table set up in the hallway, candles flickering and classical music playing, the jokey, ironic attempt at 'adult' sophistication. I remember one of them sighing and saying '*Voilà! The ubiquitous ratatouille . . .*' as she placed the heavy orange casserole pot on the table. I had never had ratatouille before. Digging among the tomato and peppers I fished something out and tried to eat it. Moments later, my cheeks burning as I picked strands of string and fibre from my teeth, Ally, or Hilly, explained what a bouquet garni was.

Later that night, on the chintzy sofa, I told Hilly – or Ally – that they were the first rich people I'd ever known. She laughed and took great pains to explain the difference between 'rich' and 'wealthy', telling me that her parents were doctors and that they were 'comfortable' but they had to earn a living. Being truly 'rich' meant having 'capital', not having to work. Where I came from it was difficult to imagine anyone further up the social scale than a doctor.

There were trips to the cinema to see strange new films with subtitles, strange new vegetables in the supermarket (I peeled my first clove of garlic aged twenty) and strange new concepts in the lecture theatre: Providence, the Augustins, Structuralism, Ironic Distance.

The Unreliable Narrator.

Earnest discussions in the refectory, arguments in the pub or union bar, as, for three years, the university went quietly about its sophistry, its business of transformation. One of these girls – a Hilly, an Ally, a Becky – once took my hand in the corner of a party and held my gaze with her clean green eyes – eyes that had seen nothing bad or ugly, that had seen only pleasant things and expected to see a good deal more of them – and told me that I was 'different' from the others. I wasn't 'full of shit'. I was 'interested' in other people. I 'listened'. I didn't just 'blah on about myself' all the time.

Later, in bed, she also told me that my past seemed to be a 'closed book'. I shrugged and smiled sadly and murmured the set backstory: the absentee father, the alcoholic mother, the abandonment as a toddler, the kindness of my elderly uncle. (No, my backstory hadn't required too much tweaking at all.) And she did something for me I hadn't been able to do myself. There in the warm single bed with the Welsh rain brushing at the window behind us, she wept.

My accent softened as, in and out of the lecture hall, my tongue found its way around strange new words, words that had had no place in my childhood: lunch, fresco, supper, Giotto. Croissant.

I was once William Anderson.

I graduated in 1992 with a BA in English Literature and Language. After a minor identity scare the following year (tabloid revelation, the wrong guy) I moved to Canada. It was far enough away with an English-speaking population and a large Scottish ex-pat population. I wouldn't attract much attention. I studied for my Masters at the University of Toronto. I moved to Regina for the postgraduate Journalism course. I met Sammy. Walt was born.

I am Donald Miller.

28

I STOPPED talking. I don't know how long it had
taken to get it all out. Walt was looking at me. I
could feel it, but I couldn't look at him. She was
still perched on the edge of the wooden table, her
arms folded across her chest. It was quiet for a
moment.

'Thank you,' Gill Docherty said. 'You know,
I really couldn't believe it was you at first. After
all this time?' She was moving now, walking
around the table, the knife in her hand. 'And
how you'd landed on your feet! Marrying the
rich girl? Your huge house and your fun little
househusband life. Having said that, I always
thought you'd be the one I might get. Derek
Bannerman? Sadly he'll never see the outside of
a prison cell again. Your friend Tommy? Well,
you know what happened to him and good

riddance to bad rubbish. But you, with your "model rehabilitation" . . .

'And then, having to be so patient this last year? Getting your trust. Waiting for the perfect time. After I had my first winter here last year I knew, I knew the weather might give us the privacy we'd need. You see, I thought about just abducting Walt here. But your father-in-law's money . . . it could have made things difficult. Besides, I wanted you to watch.'

'Please. Just kill me. Let Walt go.'

'Kill you?' She laughed here. She actually laughed. 'I'm not going to kill you.' She crossed behind Walt's chair and started pushing him in towards the table. Walt started screaming behind his gag, struggling against the ropes.

'Oh please, oh God . . .'

She banged his chair up against the table and untied his right arm, flattening his hand down on the rough wooden surface, her hand over his tiny one. Walt strained and pushed and twisted against his bonds. She picked up the hunting knife. I couldn't hear what Walt was screaming behind the gag but I knew what it was – *'Daddy! Daddy!'*

'NO!' I was screaming. 'DON'T!'

She put the tip of the blade against the wood in front of Walt's hand and brought the heel of the knife up above his pinkie. 'Walt?' she said to my son. 'Remember, everything that is going to happen to you tonight is because of your dad. He did this to you. OK?' Walt was struggling, trying to say something. Through my own tears and screams I flashed on when Walt was born, the howling blob of gore wrapped in a hospital blanket, the desire to protect and nurture – unfathomable, depthless.

Then she was bringing the heel of the blade down and, blissfully, I was fainting, the basement dissolving away into murk, but I could hear her talking, standing over me, holding my hair, telling me something.

29

YOU KNEW you should never have sent him to that school. You'd argued about it. But, in the end, Stephen had prevailed. With his new job, the pay cut, the mortgage to pay, the fees at Hutchinson were out of the question. So off to Ravenscroft he went, your perfect, special wee boy. It used to break your heart to sit in the car, the old blue Triumph Dolomite, and watch him walk through those gates, through the scowling throng of boys who towered over him, the boys who were forever spitting on the ground. The kind of boys for whom school was prison, a sentence to be endured before real life could begin, real life for most of them being, at best, a job on the production line somewhere. Factory fodder.

Not for Craig. Always bright, always interested in things. He could hold a conversation when he was nine months. Read at three.

He'd been a difficult birth. Nearly killed you. Forty hours in labour before they had to perform an emergency Caesarean. Then the complications, the return to surgery, the hysterectomy. But you had Craig. And you were so happy for a while, the three of you.

Before that school.

You'd find Craig in his room, with his homework books, taking him his milk and sandwich, and you'd know he'd been crying. The time he came home with the black eye and bruised, cut face. You'd gone berserk. Went to see the headmaster, even though Craig begged you not to, and got the boy that did it suspended. You'd wept and he'd held you, your little boy, and said, 'Don't cry, Mummy.' After that you knew he wasn't telling you everything that happened at school. (You realised much later it was because he didn't want you to worry about him, and the pain of that realisation, of his consideration, after he was dead was more than your mind could bear. Already buckled, it snapped in half.)

That May Saturday, the anxiety building within you as afternoon bled into early evening and then into nightfall and he still didn't come home. Vomiting with fear. Then the drive to the police station, Stephen patting your hand while he drove, saying,

'It'll be fine, it'll be fine. He'll have got lost.' And you already knowing, knowing something terrible had happened. The days that followed; a numbness, constant trembling, looking at the phone, watching the TV, the press conference and flashbulbs and people asking stupid, inane questions. ('How do you feel?') Then that moment – life ending – when the police car pulled up in front of the house that Thursday morning and you saw them walking up the drive, past the reporters who had gathered at the gate every morning for the last three days. You saw the expression of the lead policeman and you saw something in it beyond sorrow, beyond anxiety and nerves, you saw *fear* and that could only mean one thing.

Stephen screamed when they told you both.

You remember falling to your knees on the carpet, next to the coffee table, the world rushing around you, colours and smells seeming to intensify madly – the late daffodils on the table bright and pungent. The policeman's shoes close to your face – boot polish and leather – as you folded in on yourself, shaking.

How well you would remember the events of that last morning together in the years to come. You'd replay every moment, bringing out details, burnishing them, making them shine, making your pain so severe it felt like you would burst sometimes.

As it was the weekend, you'd all had a leisurely breakfast together: boiled eggs and toast and tea for you and coffee for Stephen, Craig with his soldiers (he was growing out of it but you still liked to do it) and orange juice. That spot of yolk on his bottom lip, you can see it still, shining in the spring sunshine that flooded the kitchen. Radio Clyde on in the background, Stephen with the sports pages of the *Herald* and you with the news.

He went to his room after breakfast to do some homework. That was the kind of wee boy you had – one who would do homework, unasked, on a Saturday morning. You popped your head round his door a little later to ask what he wanted in his sandwiches; cheese and ham, or just ham? He was at his desk, books and jotters spread out around him. 'Just ham please,' he'd said. (Did he? Did he say 'please'? He often did, but not always. You so want that 'please' to have been there in this exchange.)

He loved to go fishing in the spring and summer months. Stephen had always taken him when he was small but, just in the past year, since turning thirteen, he'd been allowed to go on his own as long as he was back well before dusk fell. And he was. He always was.

You'd put the sandwiches in a Tupperware box and packed them in his canvas knapsack along with a carton of juice and a KitKat.

Your last motherly duty.

They fished the knapsack out of the river later, not far from his body. The sandwiches were still dry and uneaten, safely waterproofed in their plastic box. There was a ball of tinfoil in the knapsack too. He'd eaten the chocolate quickly, unable to wait. You often picture him doing this: breaking a finger off and munching it as he walked along the riverbank with his rod. Had he just finished eating it, you couldn't help wondering, when he met them? Was there thick chocolate coating his tongue, bits of wafer between his teeth, when he came round the bend at that weir? He hadn't been eating it when he met them, you knew that much. That ball of tinfoil, you knew it was from the KitKat wrapper – he hadn't just thrown it on the ground like so many boys his age would have. If he'd been eating it when he met them he wouldn't have had enough time to ball up the tinfoil and put it in his knapsack. He hadn't littered. For many years, remembering just this detail would be enough to tear you apart, to have you pouring an extra inch or two of vodka into your glass.

Not that Craig was perfect of course. He'd reached an age where his intelligence was beginning to outstrip your own and this occasionally brought out a sarcastic streak in him. He could be verbally witty, but he hadn't yet learned to use it appropriately. More and more you'd found yourself having to tell him off for being cheeky. Stephen was more relaxed about it, feeling that by the time he was sixteen or seventeen he would be a formidable conversationalist, a shoo-in for the sixth-form debating team, which would look good on his UCCA form.

He wasn't sure what exactly he wanted to do yet – he loved science, he especially adored his physics teacher Mr Cummings – but Stephen was already talking excitedly about Craig going to Glasgow University, where he had gone. About how the two of you would go up and visit him: lunches on Byres Road, walks through Kelvingrove Park and the leafy Gothic quads in the autumn of first term, Craig's first term, October 1987. 'Och,' you would say, 'he's only thirteen. Let's see how his O levels go first . . .'

The trial, those three boys, bored, nervous and smirking in the dock. The details that emerged.

Splinters of fibreglass in his rectum.

Five days in the cold salty water.

Your baby boy.

'Full fathom five thy son lies; of his bones are coral made: those are pearls that were his eyes.'

Fish feeding on the blood and viscera. Burrowing inside him. Flies laying their eggs inside him, maggots ripening in his flesh, in the beautiful smooth skin you used to bury your face in, tickling him, inhaling his baby perfume. Rats gnawing at him as he floated face down in the dun river. His expression as those boys beat and whipped him and he looked up and felt the incredible degree of cruelty ranged against him. How he must have screamed when they . . .

And you do this every night. Every hour. He dies again and again. New details are imagined and added. Every night Craig screams for you to help him and you just sit and watch.

So. You go insane. Little by little you go completely insane.

In a way it was better for you. You just shut down. You stopped living. You'd be clearing away the breakfast things in the kitchen and your legs would buckle beneath you. You'd sit down on the floor, your back against the wall, and the next thing you knew the front door would be opening and Stephen would walk into the kitchen with his briefcase and you'd look up, blinking, and realise it was five o'clock. The afternoons alone in the house with the baby pictures, making him live again in your head. Making him walk and talk for you. Laughing and clapping when he did something funny or great.

It was worse for Stephen. He tried to cope more like a man. He kept working and tried to compartmentalise. Drink was involved for him right away. Not for you until later. You found the bottle of Whyte & Mackay in the boot of the car. The half-bottle in his briefcase. You blamed Stephen of course. The school fees argument replayed all the time in your head. If only. We should have. If and should and if and should on and on in a loop.

And then that morning, the week before Easter 1984, the second Easter without Craig (he'd have been fifteen), when you woke early and Stephen wasn't in bed. But that wasn't so unusual because he was sleeping so little by that point. You went downstairs into the kitchen, where the kettle was still slightly warm but the tea was going cold in the pot, like he'd made it and forgotten about it. There was a stillness to the house, even though it was much too early for him to have left for work.

Then you noticed the door that led through the

utility room and out to the garage was open. Twelve footsteps – all it took for you to reach the garage door. You opened it and there he was, Stephen Docherty, your husband, twisting gently in a slow circle, his feet just a few inches off the ground, the little white stepladder on its side. The puddle of urine beneath him. He had no shoes on and he'd used a length of blue nylon clothes line, tied it around one of the beams. You didn't cry right away, just stood there with your pupils widening and widening in the murky wooden light, listening to the gentle creak, creak, creak, the sound of rope against beam, reminding you of a hammock, of sailing ships. His face as purple as a raw heart, his mad tongue.

You'd been married eighteen years.

You thought you might be OK because Stephen had taken out fresh life insurance just before Craig died. You remembered that night – the insurance agent's aftershave sweet and coconutty in the front room, Stephen bending over the papers, wearing his glasses as he signed with a flourish, as men often do. You didn't know – why would you? – that suicide within two years of taking out the policy automatically invalidates it. If he had just stuck with the old policy everything would have been fine. This wasn't even irony, just another scene in the horror film that your life had become. Your lawyers argued your case with the insurance company – the extreme stress and trauma you'd been through – and finally they relented and agreed to a compromise payment, issuing a cheque for £1,048.00. 'Without prejudice.' It didn't even cover the lawyers' and undertakers' bills.

You had to sell the home you loved so much.

And that was how, in 1987, you found yourself turning forty alone in a two-bedroom council flat near the harbour. You discovered drink yourself then. Wine was the first thing. You found you could scrape through the day until around five o'clock before uncorking a bottle of sweet white wine. You'd never been much of a drinker and just two or three glasses of musky Riesling, or sugary Liebfraumilch, would make the shabby little flat seem warmer, homelier. The bottle would see you through until ten, when you fell asleep on the sofa, running eagerly into the dreams where Craig and Stephen were waiting for you, your arms flung wide and love pouring out of them like light. Then five o'clock became four o'clock. One bottle became two. Soon enough you were drinking from noon till bedtime. It was taking a bottle to have the effect a glass used to have.

Such a revelation when you discovered spirits.

That a half-glass of vodka had the same effect as half a bottle of wine! And in an instant! You felt like you'd split the atom. Found penicillin in the gunk at the bottom of the Petri dish. Pretty soon it was taking a bottle of Smirnoff to get you through the day. At your bedroom window you could just see the sea, the mouth of the river, before it snaked inland, where Craig's body had been found. ('Full fathom five thy son lies . . .') You'd sit there for hours, sipping neat vodka, the fumes tearing your eyes, watching the sea, the drifting white cauliflower clouds against the grey sky, singing little songs to yourself. You found yourself sitting inside your wardrobe one morning, already drunk at ten o'clock, giggling with Craig's red sweater draped over your face, inhaling him in your red tent, and you realised you were going mad, that you had gone mad, but there was a quiet detachment about it, the alcohol like a liquid pane of double-glazing, keeping you apart from the blue rage in your soul.

30

I CAME round. I had no idea how long I'd been unconscious but she'd bandaged Walt's hand in that time: a thick white dressing covering most of it, a dark patch of black blood visible where his pinkie used to be. She'd wiped up most of the blood. I started retching again, dry racking heaves. There was nothing left to come up.

'Now, William,' she said, moving in front of me. Walt's head was lolling, I wasn't sure if he was conscious or not. 'What are we going to do with you? I'm still not sure that you're telling me the whole truth. I thought you would have, given the display we've just had . . .' She gestured to Walt with the knife, gouts of dried blood were caught between the serrated teeth. 'In court you all blamed each other, didn't you? No one ever came right out and said, "I did it." The other two blamed you, didn't they? And I always wondered about you. You always struck me as clever. Slippery.'

'It was Banny.'

'Hmmm. Maybe we can incentivise you further . . .' She moved towards her bag and then stopped, her head tilting upwards, towards the wooden ceiling. It came again and I heard it too, a faint pinging, like a microwave.

The doorbell.

She turned and looked at me as it came again. She bent down, speaking right into my face as she tied the gag back into place. 'If you're thinking of doing anything stupid on the basis that it can't get any worse for you . . .' She stepped back and brought the knife up, pressing the tip against my nose. 'Believe me it can. Do you understand me, William?'

I nodded.

'Good. And try not to be sick again while you're gagged. Don't want you dying on me.'

She slipped the knife into its sheath and shoved it down the back of her jeans. She picked up a big, chromed revolver from one of the workbenches – Danko's, or Hudson's, I guessed – and stuck it down the front, covering it with the baggy sweater. Before she started up the stairs she checked her reflection in a small mirror hanging on the bare brick wall. She tutted and, with the air of a woman in evening dress fixing a stray hair before heading out to the opera, wiped a streak of Walt's dried blood from her cheek. Her boots clattered up the wooden steps, a bar of light spilled briefly down the stairs, and she was gone.

Walt's mutilated right hand was still untied.

31

'MMMMFF!' I strained against the gag. 'UNNNN!' Slowly Walt looked up at me, confused, drugged-looking, in shock. His eyes were just . . . rinsed with tears, raw, terrified. I jerked my head, nodding frantically towards the table, begging him to follow me. Finally he turned and looked.

The tiny silver scalpel, right there on the table, near the edge.

'UNNNN!' *Please, Walt, understand.* It was only a couple of feet away from his bandaged right hand. Upstairs I could hear her footsteps clacking away across wooden boards. I rocked my chair from side to side, managing to inch it a fraction closer to Walt's, watching the baby monitor. 'UNNNN!' Finally he understood, his eyes going from mine to the scalpel. He reached out. As he did so a spasm of pain seemed to shoot through him and he cried

out behind his gag. The bloodstain on the bandage
seemed to spread, Walt crying, shaking his head. I
looked him in the eye and tried to say everything
with only my eyes – *please, son, I know this hurts, but
if we don't get out of here, we will die.*

He tried again, his shoulders shaking as he cried,
blood from his wound smearing across the wooden
arm of the chair as his trembling fingertips inched
closer to the silver blade. I could faintly hear voices
from upstairs, from where she was talking to
someone at the front door.

Walt got the scalpel. He brought it back and
held it upright in his bloody, trembling fist. I
strained and pushed and pulled and rocked my
chair from side to side, squeaking and jolting and
moving it closer to Walt's, my tethered left wrist
now just inches from the blade. Sweat was pouring
down my face, sweat and blood running salty into
my eyes and my mouth. I kept glancing towards
the baby monitor. How close could she be to the
listening unit? Just an inch or two more . . .

I felt a calf muscle strain and then tear as, with
a loud squeak of wood against concrete, I managed
to push my chair the final inch or two and the
scalpel touched against the rope. Walt moved the
blade back and forth and – thankfully – it was as
sharp as it looked. The twine of the grey rope came

apart instantly and in a couple of seconds my arm sprang free. I grabbed the scalpel from Walt and started slashing at the ropes binding my ankles to the chair, my other arm, cutting myself a couple of times in the process, but frantic, beyond caring.

I had Walt's legs free and was sawing through the rope around his left arm when a single loud report cracked through the house above us, followed a half-second later by the bang of something heavy hitting the floor. I tore Walt out of the chair and pulled his gag off. 'Daddy! My hand!' I plastered my palm across his mouth and nodded towards the baby monitor. Carrying Walt I stumbled across the room to the tiny, shoulder-high casement window. Outside, snow was piled halfway up the pane; black night sky filled the other half, studded with slanting snow. I grabbed the handles and tried to force the window up but it wouldn't budge an inch, jammed tight, maybe fifteen coats of paint, thirty-odd years' worth, sealing it up. I heard her footsteps somewhere above us, getting louder, and I clutched the tiny scalpel in my fist, looking towards the steps. Then the footsteps receded again, growing fainter, and I heard a smooth, slithering sound – something heavy being dragged across wooden floorboards.

I turned back to the window and jammed the

scalpel into thick paint sealing up the bottom edge. I began drawing it across from left to right, working it into the cut I was making, pushing hard. Decades of gummy cream paint cracked and flaked off. Walt hugged into my leg, shaking, terrified. I had the scalpel a little over halfway across and could feel movement, some give in the left-hand side of the window, when there was a twanging *CRACK!* I looked down at the stump of the scalpel handle I was holding, the blade snapped off, lost inside the window. 'Shit!' I strained with both hands, trying to push it up, but the right-hand side was still gummed, stuck solid. I rammed my shoulder hard, one, two, three times against the frame. I looked at the baby monitor.

Fuck it.

I took a step back and threw myself up at the frame. Glass smashed and wood splintered as it came free, cold air hitting my face as I slid it up.

From upstairs we heard her breaking into a run.

'Hurry, Daddy!' Walt screamed.

I lifted Walt up and pushed him through the gap, out into the freezing, stinging night. Behind me I heard wood smashing against brick as she kicked the cellar door open. A split second to decide.

Stay and try and fight her?

If she shoots you, she gets Walt.

As her feet came clattering down the wooden steps I grabbed both sides of the window casement, looking like a man launching himself on a bobsleigh run, and hurled myself at the narrow gap as, behind me, I heard her enraged scream, the boom of the gun and a windowpane beside my head exploding.

Then I was picking Walt up and trying to run through knee-deep snow, the black air freezing, wind whipping our faces, and my mind still giving its own detached commentary — *She won't be able to get through that gap. She'll have to go back upstairs and through the house, buying you maybe sixty seconds. Your house, that gun in your desk drawer, is nearly half a mile away, through* — as another loud crack rang out and I turned to see her; half hanging out of the tiny window, her gun arm flailing as she fired wildly and then she disappeared inside, yellow light spilling out across the snow.

We had come to the front corner of the house. A porch ran all the way round the building at shoulder height and the area for about ten feet all around her property was brightly lit by the porch lights. Beyond that it was blackness. In the distance I could see the lights of our house glowing softly: my office. The desk. The gun. 'Walt, jump on my back and hold on.' I grabbed the railings and pulled the two of us up onto the porch. The porch was covered, there was no snow, nothing to leave tracks in. I crawled round the corner of the house, keeping below window level, looking up through the window of her sitting room and seeing her coming charging down the hallway, heading for the front door. I clutched Walt to me and pressed against the side of the house as we heard the front door slamming open, her feet banging down the steps. I turned and carried Walt in a low crouch, running along the side of the building and round the corner to the back. I peeked around and saw her running back and forth in front of the house, frantic, confused, pointing the gun off into the night.

Going against every instinct in my being I pushed the back door open and crept back into the house, into the kitchen. The lights were off and in the darkness I felt my trainer splash in something thick and sticky. There, on the linoleum floor, in a pool of black blood, was a body. Edging closer, pressing Walt's face to my chest, I saw it was Jan Franklin, part of her face missing. *She must have popped into ours to find out what had been going on with the helicopter. Had she seen the bodies there? Why had she come here? The phone?* 'Don't look, Walt.' I stepped around the blood, scanning the room, part of me hoping to see a gun rack, a shotgun on the table. Nothing. Just an ordinary, tired, old suburban kitchen. I could hear her shouting our names now from the front. I looked out the kitchen window. That pool of light extending ten feet or so into the snow, darkness beyond it, a big pine just on the edge of the darkness. If we ran into the snow she'd see our tracks right away. I looked up at the roof of the porch, trying to think, trying to remember the layout of her house from the few times I had been there. I made a decision.

Carrying Walt I ran upstairs; crouching down in the dark house as we came to the first landing I saw her through a side window, running around the house, the big revolver gripped tightly in her fist, scanning the snow. A North Face jacket, black, thickly padded, lay on a chair on the landing and I grabbed it and wrapped it around Walt. A big picture window in front of us led out onto the roof of the porch. I opened it very gently and slid it up as quietly as I could and climbed out. I saw her run out into the snow, almost directly below us. 'WILLIAM!' she yelled into the night. I pressed back, hugging the darkness and watched as she ran on around the house. The porch roof was wide, maybe ten feet or so, enough for maybe three strides in terms of a run-up. Could I make it, carrying Walt? 'Walt? Walt? Listen, son.' I pressed my mouth to his ear. 'We're going to have to jump,

OK? Just hang onto me. Hang on really tight, OK?'
He made a noise, a whimper, and wrapped his legs
around my waist even tighter, his arms clutching
around my neck.

I backed up to the wall of the house and took a
deep breath. If I came up short – we were dead.
If the snow wasn't deep enough to break our fall,
if I broke my leg or my hip – we were dead. I
glanced back through the window, along the hall
and out the window at the front of the house. I
could just hear her shouting, screaming now. I ran,
managing one, two, three powerful strides before
I came to the edge and leapt off into the night,
throwing us forward, trying to get as far into the
snow as possible, aiming for just left of the pine
tree. A split second of silence, falling through the
sleeting snow, and then, with a heavy crump, we
came down, sinking down three or more feet into
it, freezing, shocked, but safe. I scrambled around
and looked back.

We'd landed in the darkness beyond the lights.
If you were standing on the porch looking out
you'd see no sign of any tracks. I gathered Walt to
me and pressed us down into the snow, watching
the house. A burst of light as the kitchen windows
lit up and I could see her in there, not thirty feet
away – opening drawers, throwing things out,

looking for something. A gust of wind above us and the snow started to fall even harder, huge thick flakes pouring down, melting through my hair, numbing my head, Walt wriggling beneath her jacket, me becoming sickeningly aware of the sweetness of her perfume in the fur collar.

She ran back out of the kitchen door and a white cone of torchlight cut through the night, snowflakes catching dazzling in it as she jerked the beam around, scanning randomly into the blackness beyond the porch lights. She gripped the rail and stared out into the night. 'WHEN I FIND YOU,' she howled. 'I'M GOING TO CASTRATE BOTH OF YOU!'

She ran off again, back around the porch to the other side. When she disappeared I picked up Walt and started walking, pushing my way through thigh-deep snow, away from the house and off into the night, into the blizzard.

32

GOING INSANE was, obviously, a strange thing to experience. You always thought that if it happened to you you'd be conscious of it happening; that a part of your mind would still be capable of remaining aloof, aloft, of standing there and commenting on it, of saying, 'Well, this is unusual, but we seem to be doing it anyway.' But it wasn't like that at all, that day in the frozen-food section of the Safeway, when that lady – Isobel something – who you knew from your drama club put her hands on your shoulders and started speaking to you. You could see her lips moving but you couldn't make out any words. No. What you did notice was that she was crying. You looked over her shoulder and saw your reflection in the smoked-grey plastic door of a freezer containing many types of frozen chips (your mind already automatically saying, 'Oh, the boys like those ones with their gammon . . .'). You were wearing your pyjamas and a dressing gown. There were various stains down the front – egg, some blood maybe – and your hair . . . Jesus, your hair. You had long since stopped going near a mirror in the flat. Unwashed in God knows how long, it was like greased straw, sticking out in tufts and bunches, plastered to your face with sweat and tears. Looking down you saw the contents of the basket you didn't even know you were carrying – a litre of Smirnoff, an air-freshener, some birdseed – you had no birds! – and Findus Crispy Pancakes, minced beef flavour (Craig's favourite). You saw now that the supermarket manager and a security guard were standing off to the side, nervously watching Isobel talking to you (you could make out some of her words now: 'Oh Gill, oh dear God, hen. What have you done to yourself?') and the realisation hit you quietly, softly: 'Oh, I see. I've forgotten I was insane and I've accidentally wandered out in public.' It was as though insane was something it was perfectly acceptable to be behind closed doors. As long as you kept it to yourself, what was the problem? They called an ambulance and you can't really remember what happened after that. There might have been talk of having you sectioned but it never happened. Resources, you imagined.

And all the time, on the sofa, or lying on the carpet or the kitchen floor (you didn't really go to bed any more, you just passed out wherever you happened to be, babbling the songs you used to sing to him when he was a baby: there were three little fishes in a little bitty pool and there were two little boys with two little toys and one man went to mow), you fantasised about how it would happen, how it would go.

A gun would be the best thing. A friend of Stephen's – Alan something – had a shotgun. Single bore you remembered from when they'd gone out to hunt rabbits one time, down the shore at dawn. You wondered about where he kept it, how you could get it. The icy impersonal steel of the barrel in your mouth. Could you reach the trigger easily that way? Would you need a stick or something to press it? And then – just nothing. Just the back of your skull blowing up and all the billions of thoughts fizzing out in a pink mist, spattering porridgy on the walls, the curtains, the ceiling. Everything in there – Craig, Stephen – atomised. But you wouldn't even know about that.

The sharp agonising bang the metal rails would make – on your forehead, on your knees – for a split second before the howling roar of the train made everything go away. (Would you feel it? you wondered disinterestedly. The wheels as they popped your head off. Severed your legs.)

The whooshing rush of cold air as you leapt from the top of the high flats; twenty storeys passing by. Old ladies looking out their windows seeing your dark shape flash past. You reckoned the drop would take around two seconds. Would you pass out? You'd heard people do. Would you feel it? Your whole body bursting open like a sac of blood.

The razor scraping against the wrist bone, horrible and alien, like polystyrene squeak and blackboard nails. The spurt your blood would make into the hot water; flowing thick and syrupy; terrible red bath gel, the kind of gift Craig would get you sometimes, from Boots in the mall. The Christmas gift set. Then everything getting warm and fuzzy and faraway, your chin slipping under the line, your own blood sweet in your mouth, fragrant in your nostrils.

Or like Stephen – the moment of no return as the stool clattered away beneath you, your feet lashing skittishly out, flailing for purchase. The rope bristling and ticklish as it cut into your neck, feeling your tongue swelling, filling your mouth, saliva spilling down your chin, your eyes bulging. Would you scrabble at the noose, realising too late you'd changed your mind? Would you still be conscious to feel the warm urine spreading down your thighs?

The salty Firth of Clyde filling your lungs when you could swim no further. Your clothes sodden and heavy as they dragged you down. And you were still strong. A strong swimmer. You'd make it quite far out. There were nuclear submarines out there in the Clyde estuary off the Ayrshire coast. You saw them all the time. Would you float down past one of those monsters? Tumbling weightless and dead past its gigantic black metal flank, its awful conning tower alone almost as big as one of the high flats. Its churning propeller sucking you towards it, the propeller the diameter of a house and deafening, the sound amplified underwater.

You remembered Craig explaining his physics homework to you once; how the force of an explosion was greatly magnified underwater. Something to do with the density of water itself. You'd been peeling potatoes, trying to get something into the oven, and you hadn't really given him your full attention.

You would gladly undergo all of the deaths you'd imagined, all the deaths you could ever imagine, and more, many, many more, one after the other, just to have five minutes with him, just to put the fucking potato peeler down and listen to him talk about his homework.

Drunk, flying, you'd get all your cuttings out and pore over them: Craig's face on the front page of the *Daily Record*. 'MISSING!' Photos of the frogmen on the banks of the river. Those silhouettes – Boys A, B and C. Then, later, after the Home Secretary's ruling, the photos of Derek Bannerman (14), Thomas McKendrick (13) and William Anderson (13).

How you stared at these, tracing your finger over their faces, imagining, projecting.

The 1990s came and went and that might well have been it. Your life. Dead from cirrhosis in your fifties.

And then something happened.

It had been so long since you'd experienced good fortune that it took you a while to recognise it for the blessing, the opportunity it was.

Just after the millennium, Stephen's Aunt Myra died. She'd lived in Inverness and you'd never met her. A spinster, Stephen had been the only living relative. The estate had been considerable, one of those old ladies with two houses and fifteen bank books under the bed. A cheque came via the lawyers for £180,000. You celebrated with a case of Smirnoff Blue Label.

Waking a few mornings later, fully clothed on

the sofa, empty bottles and full ashtrays, dried sick on your navy cardigan, you had your very own 'moment of clarity'.

Certainly you could use this money to quickly drink yourself to death. Or . . .

You could use it to try and get back what had been taken from you. Justice. Restitution. Vengeance. Whatever the world wanted to call it.

You poured the rest of the vodka down the toilet and you never drank again. You became something you never imagined yourself being.

A detective.

33

I STILL do not fully understand how I managed to do what I did that night. The stories you hear about the drugs that lie dormant within the human body, the kind of super-adrenalins that make it possible for women to lift cars off infants, for people to outswim pursuing sharks? They're surely true.

My right leg throbbed from the impact with the ground. I had Walt, all sixty pounds of him, thrown over my shoulder, wrapped up in the North Face jacket, some of it covering my front as I stumbled further into the snow. My feet and legs were soaked, all extremities numb. I blinked as the snow stung my face, sweat and freezing water running into my eyes. Minus eighteen, easily. I had no real idea where we were heading, just trying to put more and more distance between us and her, the snow a godsend in one way; it was falling so fast

it was covering our tracks. Walt cried and whim-
pered into my neck as I repeated 'It's OK. It's going
to be all right' whenever I had the breath, my
temples throbbing, my mind wandering randomly,
crazily, as I gradually fell into a trance-like state.

I was William Anderson again, back in Scotland,
back at school, Banny's face looming out of the
dark and snow in front of me, huge and terrible
and sneering, Banny whispering to me, telling me
terrible things, saying *'you were always a wee fanny'*,
saying *'ma da fucked me up the erse'*. Tommy too; his
throat gashed wide open, blood pouring from the
corners of his mouth, his eyes just whites, no pupils,
no irises, just white, awful blanks as he laughed his
short, cruel, barking laugh. I saw my parents
floating in front of me, sitting wordlessly in front
of a television, my dad's King Billy tattoo, snatches
of the Orange songs he used to sing when he was
drunk flickering through my head, *'He was halfway
up a nun, when King Billy shot his gun,'* and then the
song was morphing into Duran Duran, into 'Hungry
Like the Wolf', and Herby was bounding towards
us through the snow, a barrel with 'XXX' stamped
on it, like in the cartoons, like on *Glen Michael's
Cavalcade* I used to watch on Sunday mornings when
I was wee, but then Herby got closer and I saw

that he'd been cut in half — just the front half of a dog crawling towards us, the front paws pulling the whole thing along, an awful slick of blood trailing in his wake through the snow. And then, suddenly, we were surrounded by sunshine and clear spring air and I was back on that riverbank, almost thirty years ago, but this time I had a gleaming revolver in my hand, pointing the gun at Banny, and this time I could stop it all, make him stop, make me stop, and I was pointing the gun at Banny but he just walked towards me as I pulled the trigger and the bullets (*the buttels, Walt, the buttels*) just dropped feebly out of the barrel, tinkling harmlessly onto the concrete, but it was warm and sunny and I felt drunk, happy, delirious and I knew, knew it now . . .

I was dying of hypothermia.

I collapsed into the snow, Walt falling down on top of me, his weight beneath the jacket the only warmth I had. And suddenly the instinct was impossible to resist: to roll over in the snow, to burrow down, pull the cold blanket in over us and drift off to sleep. I was no longer shivering. I lay flat on my back and stared up into the uncountable snowflakes, hugging my son to me. Walt's lips were blue, his skin almost translucent, his eyes partially open and glazed, dead. *Come on, Walt, ma wee man. Take my hand. It won't hurt, son. Let's go. Let's go and see Mommy.*

And then Craig Docherty's face appeared above us in the night sky: enormous and awful and grinning, like a star constellation floating luminous, coming down. He had no eyes at all, just great coils of pink worms, wet and writhing in the empty sockets, reaching down towards us like tendrils. A tiny crab scuttled out of his nostril and into his mouth and he was laughing.

No. We were not going to die here, in the fucking snow.

I hauled myself up, threw Walt back over my shoulder, and put one foot in front of the other.

After a few hundred stumbling, freezing yards I saw it up ahead through the blizzard. I couldn't even be sure what it was at first, thought it was another mirage, a cruel trick of psychosis. I didn't really believe it was real until I reached out and touched its cold breeze-block wall. It was our pool house and, in the distance, just a couple of hundred yards away, I saw now the weak yellow lights of the main house, just visible through the snow. We must have come nearly a mile, all the way to the back of our property. I pushed the door open and we fell in through a four-foot drift of snow.

34

SPRAWLING ON the gritty cement floor, in the workshop part of the pool house, I caught my breath as my eyes adjusted to the darkness. I could make out the shapes of machinery around me; the big petrol mower, the Bobcat snowmobile, the old barbecue set. The only light in the room was a tiny forest-green square in the corner near the floor, the 'on' light of the chest freezer. Being used only in summer the building was unheated but somewhere over there was the little plug-in electric fan heater that Danny used sometimes when he did work out here. Walt was lying on his side, breathing shallowly, his head lolling. He looked drunk. I crawled over and brought the heater back, plugging it in, turning it on, a tiny red square joining the green one in the darkness, hot air blasting over Walt.

'Walt. Walt! Can you hear me?'

'Mmmm.'

'We're in the pool house. I've got the heater on. Stay here. I'm going to get some towels.'

Feeling my way in the darkness, my breath misting in front of me, I went through the connecting door that led to the changing-room half of the structure and found some dry towels stacked on the pine benches. Lying on the floor, as I'd hoped, I found a pair of Walt's old combat pants and a couple of T-shirts, all stale and dirty but dry. I locked the exterior door that led from the pool-side into the changing room. I glanced through a dirty, frosted windowpane towards the main house. The lights were still on at the back of the house, the corridor that ran along the bedrooms. Beyond getting Walt warm and dry I had only one thought: get to the office and get my gun. Then I saw a red shape moving fast past one of the windows and I dropped to my knees below the window.

She was in the house.

She was waiting for us. Maybe waiting until the storm abated a little, or for the first rays of daylight, so she could go out on the Bobcat and make sure we were dead, find our bodies somewhere in the snow. I ran back through to Walt in a low crouch. He was shivering again, a good sign. I checked his hand, having to stifle the sobs in my chest, and saw that the bandage was iced up, crusted to him with frost, but that he'd stopped bleeding. I towelled him dry, stripped his wet clothes off and quickly dressed him in the dry ones. I took an ancient, filthy Barbour jacket of Danny's from a nail on the wall and wrapped him in it, pulling the wet North Face one on myself now, my skin recoiling at its slime and damp, the faint scent of her perfume still on it.

'Is that better?' I whispered.

'C . . . cold.' He opened his eyes and looked at me sleepily.

'Just stay here, close to the heater. OK, son? We're going to be OK.'

'What happened? I . . .' He seemed to remember something and went to bring his hand up. He started to sob. 'My finger . . .'

It took everything not to cry too. 'Listen, Walt, we'll get a doctor and he'll fix it all up, OK? They can do anything these days. But we need to be quiet just now.'

He stiffened in my arms. 'Where is she?'

'She . . . she's in our house. But don't worry. The police will be here soon. You just stay here. Keep quiet. Keep warm.'

'Don't go!' he almost yelled as I went to get up.

'I'm not, Walt. I just need to do something, OK? I'll be right over there.'

He nodded and I moved over to the window on my haunches.

I looked towards the house again, but there was no sign of her. I looked at my watch – nearly 2 a.m. It'd probably be first light before Regina started trying to contact the helicopter team on the radio. Five or six hours at least. Could we just crawl into a corner and wait to be rescued? *She's going to start checking these outbuildings.* The next thought followed automatically – *she's going to come through that door sooner or later and you'd better have an idea about what you're going to do.*

I scanned the workshop: some garden tools, shears, a rake, spades. A crate of empty wine bottles, from a party last summer. Nothing you'd want to go up against a handgun with. The mower, the snowmobile, a shelf of tools – chisels, pliers, spanners, a three-pound hammer I'd last used to drive the post for the Swingball set into the grass. A box of Cook's Matches next to the barbecue.

The matches triggered a string of connections.

Matches, bottles, mower.

I leaned down, unscrewed the cap and sniffed the mower's tank. Using a sharp chisel I cut a length of garden hose off the big green reel. I lowered it into the tank, put the end in my mouth and sucked, instantly getting a mouthful of petrol, gagging and coughing, memories of a summer night nearly thirty years ago flooding through me. I retched and spat and then filled an empty wine bottle. I tore a strip from one of the towels, soaked it with petrol, and stuffed it into the neck of the bottle. All the while Walt lay in the corner by the softly whirring heater, quietly watching me, not speaking. I took the box of Cook's Matches from the barbecue, pulled a packing crate up to the little window and sat down, stuffing the three-pound hammer into my belt. (If things went wrong, if the worst came to the worst, I hoped the first blow would stun Walt completely, that the second or third would kill him.)

'The past is another country' runs the hoary old cliché. I thought mine was another aeon, another planet. *I was a wee boy who did a terrible thing.* But the past isn't another country. It is ever-present. It was out there now, somewhere in the snow, with a butcher's knife and a heavy revolver.

I waited.

The snow finally stopped.

35

IT WAS perhaps thirty minutes after the snow stopped that I saw it – a white-yellow cone of light scything through the dark. I moved closer to the window and watched her walk along our back porch, just visible in her red parka. The beam of her flashlight swept across the backyard, picking out the shapes of garden furniture buried under rifts of snow, moving over the outbuildings; the stables, the pergola, the pool house. I ducked out of the way as the cone swept along the wall, Walt whimpering in fear as it cut through the workshop, playing weakly on the walls above our heads. It moved away and I peeked out. She was heading towards the stables, the building nearest the house.

'Come on, Walt,' I whispered.

I picked him up and, crouching low, carried him through to the changing room, settling him on the floor near the door I locked earlier, out of sight of the window. 'Now just stay here and be very, very quiet. OK?'

He grabbed at my sleeve. 'No! Don't go. I'm scared.'

'Listen, son, I'm only going to be next door. I . . . please, Walt. Be brave.' I peered over Walt's head, out of the window. The torch was already bobbing away from the stables, heading towards us.

Walt choked back a sob. I looked at him, stroked his face. 'I'll come back and get you. Whatever you do – don't make any noise. I love you.' I kissed his forehead. With a whimper, he let me go.

I crawled back through to the workshop, seeing the beam coming through the windows, bouncing crazily off the walls now. I crouched down among the machinery, behind the tarpaulin-covered Bobcat, maybe twenty feet from the door, and readied myself, the wine bottle in one hand, the long match in the other. I heard a knocking at the glass. She had her face pressed up against it, scouring the room with the torch. I flattened myself closer to the cement floor. The beam disappeared, a second or two passed, and then I heard the doorknob squeak as it started to turn. For a split second I was rigid with fear, mind blank, unable to move as the door kept shuddering and banging. *Move, do it*. I set the bottle down. The door was swinging open as I struck the match.

A soft splintering of wood against sandpaper as the matchhead crumbled to pieces.

My insides tumbled.

You didn't check the fucking matches.

The torch was raking the room now as I fumbled in the box for another, spilling matches everywhere. I struck one – another dud.

And now you're going to die.

I looked up as I took a third match between trembling fingers and saw her head coming round the door, the flashlight in one hand, the gun in the other. I struck the third match and it flared as I held it straight to the petrol-soaked towelling. It went up – a streak of clear, rose-pink flame leaping six inches into the air, burning my hand, her hearing, sensing something, wheeling around towards where I was hiding, gun extended as I leapt up, the flaming bottle in my fist, my arm already drawn back like a pitcher with a fastball. She squeezed the trigger at the same moment as I screamed and hurled the Molotov cocktail with everything I had. The concussion from the gun was deafening in the small concrete space and I felt the air move beside my face as the bullet passed inches from my cheek. The bottle flew past her head, missing her, smashing on the breeze-block wall beside her.

A *whumf* as it exploded, showering her with burning petrol, her hair and parka going up instantly, her screaming and flailing, the gun going off again, blowing a hole in the roof but I was already running, back into the changing room, grabbing Walt and throwing him over my shoulder as I unlocked the other door and sprinted for the house.

Pile-driving my aching legs through the snow, I looked back and saw her come thrashing out the door. Her upper body was just a match head; blue-tipped flames arcing several feet into the air, her terrible, high-pitched screaming suddenly stopping as she threw herself face down into the snow, legs writhing and kicking. I kept going, closing the distance between us and the house.

We came in through the utility room and I kept sprinting, down the long hallway, running full tilt, Walt still over my shoulder, weightless in the adrenalin surge. I stopped, catching my breath, and glanced into the guest bedroom on my right: Officer Hudson, on her back on the oatmeal carpet beside the bed, her eyes staring sightlessly, a huge gash across her throat, a puddle of blood around her, a spray of it across the white wall above the bed. *Cut her throat while she was sleeping.* Walt screamed. 'Don't look, Walt!' I yelled, covering his face. She was stripped to the waist, wearing just a black bra. I moved closer to the body, close enough to see that her holster was empty and her radio was gone. I backed out of the room and started running again, all the way down to my office, that glass cube on the side of the house.

I grabbed the keys from the Ramones mug, spilling pens and paper-clips everywhere, and, with shaking hands, opened the drawer and pulled out the automatic, my fingers lacing around the chequered grip and through the trigger guard, relief flooding through me.

'Daddy!' Walt cried from behind me. 'Look!'

I turned and followed his finger, through the blue-tinted glass, across the yard, to where the workshop door was swinging open in the wind, flames still flickering and licking around the door-frame, to an indented shape where she'd fallen in the snow.

She was gone.

The lights went out.

36

I CLICKED the safety off. 'Stay here,' I said to Walt. 'Under the desk.'

I crawled down the corridor and into the main living area, slithering softly across the polished wood on my stomach, the gun held in both hands in front of me, the house in total darkness around me. There were no external doors or windows that could be opened behind us; to get to where we were she would have to come from the other side of the house and cross the huge living room, fifty feet, easily. She would either come from the hallway that led down to the bedrooms and basement or the short half-staircase that led up to the kitchen. There was just enough moonlight coming through the acres of glass to see by. My hands trembled as I swung the gun from one entrance to the other, waiting. When she appeared I was going to let her get out into the open and then I was going to empty the fucking gun at her.

A noise from the kitchen – a distant, agonised cry, like pain being stifled. I tried to breathe slowly, feeling my heart flexing against the floorboards. Minutes passed in silence. Five? Ten?

The kitchen door swung open at the top of the short staircase and there she was, coming hesitantly down the steps, steadying herself against the wall with her left hand, the gun still in her right. In the semi-darkness I could see that half of her head was white, like a Q-tip, and I realised what she'd been doing: bandages, gauze, antiseptic cream maybe. She knew where everything was from babysitting Walt. I let her get to the bottom of the staircase, let her take a few steps across the hardwood floor, to within thirty feet of where I lay behind a sofa, gun trained squarely on the centre of her chest now. It was utterly silent when I cocked the pistol and watched her freeze instantly. I hesitated, my finger rigid on the trigger.

'Put the gun down,' I heard myself say.

She held her hands up. Palms outwards, fingers off the weapon. 'Put it down.'

'Don't shoot, William, I'll empty it.' With one hand she flicked the chamber on the revolver open and I heard the clatter of the big brass cartridges falling on the floor and rolling away. 'I'm going to sit down,' she said. 'I'm a wee bit weak.'

I stood up as she sat down on the edge of the sofa. She'd bandaged up the left-hand side of her face. Her hair was badly singed, frazzled. 'How do I look?' she asked, eyeing me calmly, taking in my reaction. I kept the gun on her, leaning against the arm of a chair for support, my legs close to buckling beneath me. She had started humming a little song to herself, almost absent-mindedly. 'I might become a little incoherent,' she said. 'I took a few of Samantha's Percocet, you see. For the pain? I haven't taken prescription medication for many years. They're quite strong, I think.'

'Walt?' I shouted down the hallway.

'Daddy!'

'Everything's OK. Just stay where you are.'

'Ah. The good father,' she said.

'How could you? To Sammy? To Walt? You know them, they –'

'You knew Craig.'

'I WAS JUST A KID!'

Silence. She let my shout reverberate, die away in the big echoing room. 'You'll see those moments forever, won't you? They'll never leave your head. But I wonder what's worse – definitely knowing what happened or inventing your own scenario every night? I could never really get a clear picture of what happened to Craig. I'd invent it. Alter it. Change it almost every night. And you go, you know, you go mad!'

'How, after all this time, how did you find me?'

'You remember Mr Cardew, don't you?'

37

YEARS BACK there had been a flurry of press reports surrounding the release of Boy C, William Anderson, a young man now, with a new name and a new identity. You remembered him well from court. The newspapers had tried to contact you for a quote about him getting out but you were so far gone at that point.

You began by travelling up to the Mitchell Library in Glasgow every day – taking the bright orange train along the west coast, travelling over the railway bridge, looking down at the weir where Craig died, whispering a benediction to him every time – where you sat at the microfiche tables, turning the big knob and studying every report, every photograph. There were several from Anderson's release and various prison transfers: a blanketed figure emerging from a police van, being moved through photographers into Glasgow Sheriff courthouse, the snarling mob in the background. You noticed the same figure in several different photographs; a silver-haired man in his fifties, sticking close to the shrouded figure, an expression of irritation on his face as he scanned the mob of photographers jostling for a shot.

You studied his face intently, for hours, learning every line. He didn't look like a policeman. His facial expression, as you studied it over and over, it wasn't so much irritated as anxious, concerned. He had a protective arm around the crouching figure beneath the blanket. This, you came to believe as you gazed at the grainy black-and-white photographs for hour after hour, was someone from one of the 'caring' professions: a social worker perhaps, certainly someone with great reserves of understanding. Someone who could manifest sympathy for the thing under the blanket, the thing that, according to his testimony, had watched as his friend stuck a broken fishing rod into your son's rectum.

You reasoned: if he were a social worker who had worked on this type of case . . . was it possible he was now working on others? Where would such a person be found?

Very likely in and around the courthouses of Glasgow.

It was 2002, the twentieth anniversary of Craig's death, when you began your new daily routine: that bright orange train to Glasgow, canvas bag with sandwiches, flask and research books (nursing, torture) over your shoulder. The walk from Central Station along Jamaica Street, along the river and across the bridge to the Sheriff Court. There you'd sit on one of the benches, watching the comings and goings, the lawyers and police officers and the accused and their wretched families, lost in the pall of last, hurried, cigarettes in their stained, crinkled sportswear.

You watched and you read your books and this went on for nearly two years.

Rebuilding your body was a whole lot easier than rebuilding your mind. You'd put on three stone from the drinking and your jowls, bum and belly all hung fleshy and slack. Your lungs were desiccated from pack after pack of Embassy Regal, the brand you'd chosen because it was what Stephen used to smoke years ago. The first few times you tried to go running were a joke – maybe four or five hundred yards before you collapsed sobbing and panting against a hedge. But you kept going, increasing it a little every day. It must have been true that you had an addictive nature because you were soon up to three, then four, then six miles a day. From your flat you'd run the length of Harbour Street until you hit the shore, make a left on the hard, packed sand near the surf and run to Barassie and back; three miles each way along the beach, the wind whipping into you, the spray stinging your face, mixing with your sweat, burning your eyes. You'd get twitchy and irritable if you didn't get your run in by 7 a.m. and some days you'd do two runs; one first thing and another around 6 p.m., which was when you'd sometimes feel yourself getting fidgety, walking around the flat, opening the fridge door, and you knew it was your body craving a drink, wanting its old routine.

The weight fell off and you felt strength and suppleness returning. You were in your fifties and in the best shape of your life.

The town's first gym had recently opened and you started lifting weights, crunching your stomach on the rowing machine, building up your abs and pecs and your laterals. The strength in your arms and upper body grew and grew until you could pull yourself quickly up the ropes that dangled from the ceiling of the gym. And you liked that feeling – the couple of seconds where you paused, breathing hard at the very top of the rope, thirty feet above the floor, your head pressing against the roof, your biceps straining. You liked the fact you were alive and climbing that rope, towering above it instead of swinging at the end of it.

You enrolled in a tae kwon do class at the leisure centre, the Magnum, where you had taken Craig ice-skating a couple of times. (It terrified you, that ice rink – with all the vicious, glowering boys speeding round. The thought of Craig falling out there, his fingers spread on the watery ice as the twin blades came slicing towards him – and you were relieved when he said he didn't like it and didn't want to go any more.) You learned the punches and blocks and – especially – the powerful, sweeping kicks. Your instructor Keith told you you were a 'natural'.

And you couldn't say yet exactly why you were doing all of this. Just that you wanted to be . . . ready.

You took an evening class: Basic first aid.

The treatment of trauma and the preservation of life.

You joined the gun club, lying on your stomach on a mat on the rifle range at the leisure centre, squeezing off rounds from the old Martini action rifles they had. Learning the basics about more advanced weapons. You weren't sure what skills you'd need if the day ever came.

Then it happened, towards the end of 2004. It

was late autumn, your ears cold, a dewdrop on the tip of your nose, great rifts of desiccated leaves blowing by, when the silver-haired man from the photographs came down the courthouse steps, talking to two policemen. They came close to your bench (a history of medieval torture on your lap, open at a page on wheeling), close enough for you to hear the man's voice, working class, Glaswegian, and watch as he took an unfiltered Capstan Full Strength from its pack and expertly lit it with a match held in cupped fingers, the fingertips as yellow as the phone book. He was older, in his sixties now, but it was certainly him. He walked towards the underground station and you followed.

To Cowcaddens and then the short walk to the police station. You watched him signing in through the glass doors. You waited across the street and it was dark, five thirty, before he left again. You trailed him to Central Station, then the train out to Rutherglen. You watched as he disappeared into a tenement building near the station. Ground floor, right. You got close enough to read the little brass nameplate on the wooden door frame: 'P. CARDEW'.

Your heart had filled your whole chest from the moment you saw him.

For days you thought it over, gradually realising

that even greater reserves of patience were going to be called for. You felt sure that this man would have information about the boy who helped to kill your son. All you needed was a name and a city. However, if something untoward happened to P. Cardew, it might have reverberations for the new identity William Anderson had been given. Yet P. Cardew was old. In a few years, surely, he would retire. More time would have elapsed. Less attention would be paid.

In the end it took another four years. You discovered reserves of patience you did not know you had. You watched and waited and learned. He lived alone, a bachelor. (This was good.) He smoked and drank too much. (This was bad. Your greatest fear in that time was premature death: a stroke or a heart attack. Those Capstan Full Strength and the bottles of Grouse from the off-licence on Rutherglen High Street three or four times a week.) Then, finally, in the summer of 2008, the grim little retirement party in the pub in Cowcaddens. You were several tables away, with your Coke and your book. He even smiled at you once as he wove unsteadily to the toilets.

And still you waited another six months, noting with sadness the reductive curve of this man's retirement: his visits to the pub coming earlier in the day, the lunches with colleagues growing more infrequent already. His occasional visits to the Mitchell Library, your old haunt, where he read mainly social histories of Glasgow, often nodding off, his head lolling onto his chest in the great reading room. The smirks and the head-shaking of the nearby students.

Finally you could wait no more. You rang the doorbell one evening in early May 2009, almost exactly twenty-seven years to the day. He smiled kindly as he looked at you through thick glasses, the smell of cooking behind him in the tired old flat as he said, 'Can I help you, dear?'

You Maced him in the mouth.

He scrabbled at his throat as you pushed him backwards into the hall. He was trying to shout but the Mace was already constricting, burning his larynx. It would wear off. You needed him able to talk. Without fear, and in exactly the way you'd rehearsed it countless times, you slammed the door behind you and kicked his legs from under him, following him down, making sure he didn't bang his head on the floor, the knife already out of your other coat pocket and up at his jaw, tickling his jugular vein as you said, 'Do what I say and everything will be OK.'

The great pain, fear and confusion in P. Cardew's

eyes as you slipped your heavy rucksack off your shoulder and set it on the floor. As you took out the car battery.

Stronger than you'd expected, this 66-year-old man.

He held out for several hours, whether through loyalty to, or a genuine affection for, William Anderson, or whether because of some personal code of honour you were never quite sure. In the end you had the voltage up as high as you dared. Smoke was coming off his hair, out of his nose, the gag was barely muffling the screams and you had to have the television up loud to cover this. You were grateful for the thick walls of those old Victorian sandstones. Every time his eyeballs flipped upwards, vibrating in their sockets, you feared it might be the last time; that they'd never come back down again. Finally it came out, just four words, the sweetest four words you'd heard in many years. Almost as sweet as 'I love you, Mummy'.

'Donald' (gasping), 'Miller' (retching), 'Toronto', (panting), 'University' (sobbing).

You thanked P. Cardew and then dum-de-dummed a little song to yourself to drown out his pleading and bargaining as you carried him through to the bedroom, no fight left in him. The worn old dark-wood furniture, the green bedspread, an ashtray and a photograph of some nephews and nieces on the nightstand.

He gratefully drank down the mug of water with a fistful of your Valium and sank down, slackjawed with exhaustion. You tidied the flat, meticulously removing any trace of your presence. You lit one of his Capstan Full Strength and placed it between his fingers. He was deeply asleep as the unfiltered cigarette burned against the bedspread, forming a dark brown line that began smoking, then flaming.

You sat in the corner of the room and watched for as long as you dared. Long enough to see the bed and half the room engulfed in flames. He never woke up.

You closed the garden gate gently behind you, a soft marmalade glow just visible through the net curtains of the living room, something that would have looked to a passer-by like a nice fire burning in the grate.

You read the headline at Glasgow Airport two days later: 'RUTHERGLEN MAN DIES IN HOUSE FIRE'.

You scanned the details ('Paul Cardew, 66, recently retired . . . Strathclyde Police . . . highlighted the dangers of smoking in bed'), finished your coffee and boarded the flight to Toronto.

It all became much easier after that. Your acting skills. You were charming with the lady in the administration office at the University of Toronto and she riffled through the records and told you that Donald Miller, your nephew from Scotland ('wee Donnie' you called him), had indeed gradu- ated from the Masters programme in 1996. If you'd just hold on she'd see if – and wasn't that a lovely blouse you had on? – she could find the last address they mailed the alumni newsletter to and, oh yes, here we are, an apartment in Regina, Saskatchewan. The address was a few years old, so few of the students kept in touch to update their details, and how were you enjoying Canada?

In Regina, two days later. No Donald Miller listed in any of the phone books. It wasn't a big city, but you couldn't go asking around, you weren't quite sure how, exactly, you wanted to work it. You walked the streets a lot for the first few weeks, hoping you might see the adult face of that gap- toothed thirteen-year-old walking past you, but knowing that if you did you'd never recognise him. You went to the library and checked the electoral roll. Nothing there either. You moved from the hotel into a short-term rental and the weeks turned into months and you began to lose faith when kindly fate dealt you an unexpectedly wonderful hand. You were sitting in a coffee shop one morning when you picked up the copy of the *Regina Advertiser* someone had left lying in the booth across from you. Flipping through the real estate and local interest stories your eye snagged on the headline: 'MILLER'S CHOICE', then the little postage-stamp-sized photograph next it; a shyly grinning fortyish man. Then the byline at the bottom of the page – 'Donald Miller'.

You sat there for several minutes, your breath shallow through your nostrils. You had no way of connecting the man in the photograph with the boy from the front pages of almost thirty years ago. It was possible that this was an entirely different Donald Miller. But you knew, knew in your blood and in your bones, that it was him.

On a bench across from the *Advertiser*'s downtown offices you ate your sandwiches and read your book and did this day after day, until, after a week, you saw the man from the photograph coming out of the building talking to an attractive, well-dressed woman who looked a little older than he did. They stood talking in the sunshine by a cherry tree. You crossed the square and passed close enough to hear their voices. It was unmistakable; his accent had clearly undergone some work, some revision, but it was still there, clear and distinct, that Ayrshire burr.

You settled into a routine familiar to you from your Glasgow days with kindly Mr Cardew.

Watching. Waiting. Thinking.

Your disbelief when you saw where, and how, he lived. The enormous house of glass and timber, with its pool and outbuildings, its 4x4s in the drive and solar panels on the roof. The trips to what you soon learned was his in-laws' mansion. And then the joy, the utter joy, when you saw the boy, the son, skipping along the deck in the summer sun. (You were parked on a ridge half a mile away, with powerful binoculars and a map spread out on the roof in case of questions from passers-by.)

Because you had been wondering what to do. Had he been single, had there been nothing to take from him, it was very likely you would simply have abducted him, tortured him for as long as you could keep him alive, and then killed him. Now, when you saw all that he had to lose, a different plan suggested itself.

Take from him everything there was to take.

Make him watch.

Let him live.

Fate had one last favour in store for you. It had been staring you in the face for weeks too, you just hadn't noticed it until, one day, on one of your frequent drives by the Miller house, you glanced left down the drive that led to the farmhouse perhaps a half-mile from their property, their nearest 'neighbour' really, and noticed for the first time the yellow-and-red realtor's sign.

'TO LET'.

You drove back into Regina so fast you nearly crashed the car twice. On the drive your backstory formed in your head and you practised your accent. A Southern American – Georgia twang was something you felt very comfortable with. You'd got such compliments on it when you'd done *Streetcar* all those years ago, back at the Arts Centre, in another life, when you were another person. It was an accent you knew you could maintain without serious slippage for long stretches of conversation. You would practise too.

You were retired. Your husband had recently died. You wanted to paint landscapes – the view was perfect. No, you didn't mind that the house was a bit run-down, didn't mind at all. In fact, would they mind if you took a one-year lease with an option to extend and paid the first year's rental in advance? The realtor nearly fell over running to get the keys to take you for a look around.

You were nearly sick with fear that Saturday morning, the first time you went over there. Would your accent give you away? Was it possible he'd recognise you? Even after nearly thirty years and twenty pounds and a different hair colour? In the end it was the wife who was there to receive your home-made jam. She made coffee and you talked in the vast modern kitchen, with you oohing and ahhing over the house while you gave her a more elaborate version of the story you'd given the realtor. He came home just as you were leaving, trailing the kid behind him.

'Eye-reen,' you said, shyly extending your hand. (You'd decided that shyness would be part of your character.)

'Donnie,' he lied easily, smiling, taking your hand. 'Pleased to meet you, Irene. This is Walt.'

You looked down and smiled at the angelic little boy grinning up at you, half hiding behind his father's leg.

You walked home two feet off the ground. You had done it. Now it just required patience and planning.

Two of your strong suits.

38

SHE STOPPED talking. She seemed dreamy now, sleepy and faraway. 'Why did you wait so long?' I asked. I was sitting down now, in an armchair across from her, the gun still trained on her chest.

'I wanted to watch you for a while, see what you'd become.'

'What have I become?'

She shrugged. 'A decent person, I suppose. I don't really care. It doesn't change anything.' She had let her head drop down and was gently massaging her bandaged right temple. 'Well,' she sighed, 'what time is it, William?'

I looked at my watch, not taking the gun off her. 'Nearly three.'

'We'd best get on then.'

She reached down into her boot and pulled out a knife. My eight-inch Global chef's knife.

I stood up. 'If you don't put that down, I'll kill you.'

'Yes, why haven't you killed me? After what I did to your wife and child?' She sounded genuinely puzzled.

'If you —'

She was trying to stand up.

'PUT THE FUCKING KNIFE DOWN!'

She started getting to her feet. I trained the gun on her head, on the turban of bandages, the black sight on the barrel standing out stark against the white cotton, just five feet away, point-blank. I pulled the trigger.

Click.

She looked at me — her eyes suddenly very clear — and smiled. 'You think I didn't sit there every day with my binoculars watching you in your little office?'

Click.

'Watching you play cowboys with your stupid little gun? Keeping the bullets in one drawer, just in case little Walt stumbled upon it?'

Click.

My legs caving in.

'Silly boy, William.'

I brought the gun up to smash her in the head as she lunged with terrible speed, smashing into me, knocking me down onto the chair, driving the knife hard into my left thigh twisting it. I howled and tried to hit her with the pistol again but she caught my wrist with surprising strength and kept twisting the knife. I could feel it scraping the bone and I struggled to keep from fainting. I pushed her back and punched her in the face, driving my fist into the sodden latticework of bandages. She screamed now and stumbled backwards, falling onto the floor, letting go of the knife, leaving it sticking in my thigh, twanging, buried four inches deep, halfway up the blade. I could hear Walt yelling from down the hall as I threw myself forward at her but she kicked out, taking my legs from beneath me and I slammed straight down onto the floor, my left leg coming down first, the handle of the –

My scream deafening.

White light as I felt the impact push the blade all the way through my thigh, through bone and muscle, and out the other side. I felt myself losing consciousness. I sensed her above me, picking something up, something heavy from the table, and then I felt air above my skull moving, humming, and then I felt nothing.

39

I CAME round on my side on the floor of the games room. I'd been gagged and hog-tied; my hands behind my back, bound tightly to my feet which were folded up into the small of my back. The knife was gone from my thigh and she'd tied a crude tourniquet just above the wound. The leg of my jeans was soaked in blood and the pain was excruciating. The smell of wet leather as her boots stomped past me, carrying her Gladstone bag towards the pool table. I looked up and saw Walt.

He was lashed to the table, spreadeagled and crying. His head was turned towards me and I saw that he'd been gagged too, but his eyes were begging, imploring me to help him.

'Tell me, William.' Her tone was calm and conversational, 'How much do you know about torture? I'd say I'm fairly widely read on the subject.

It kept me going, all those years ago, when it looked hopeless. Fantasising, you could say. When I was keeping an eye on your Mr Cardew I'd sit in the Mitchell Library and read for hours. About the Chinese, the Russians, medieval methods versus modern ones . . .'

I heard a noise from the Gladstone bag, like something thunking against glass. 'Sometimes I think it was the only thing keeping me sane. You should count yourself lucky we have so little time. If only it could have been otherwise.' She was moving around the table as she talked. Pulling on Walt's ropes, binding him tighter. 'It would have provided some great opportunities. Scaphism for instance. Do you know about scaphism?'

She perched on the edge of the pool table, the big knife in her hand, and turned to me, talking on, oblivious to Walt crying and struggling uselessly behind her. 'It comes from the Greek "*skaphe*", meaning "scooped out", but was mainly practised in ancient Persia. What they did, those clever Persians, was they took you to a riverbank in summertime and they lashed you inside a hollowed-out tree trunk, with your head sticking out one end and your feet out the other and they let you float in the shallow water, among the reeds, while they force-fed you for a couple of days. Lord did they feed you. They made you drink so much milk and honey that you developed diarrhoea. You'd be just . . . *filling* that tree trunk up with rivers of nasty filth. They'd rub honey on your face and feet too if they really didn't like you. And then they'd leave you. Well, not completely. They'd stay to watch and feed you. Great crowds of people sometimes, clapping and cheering as you floated on the stagnant water, under the hot sun. You'd have been fairly roughly beaten up prior to all this of course, your own faeces flowing into your cuts, your mouth, your eyes. Then the insects would come. Flies and mosquitoes. Ants, wasps and beetles and whatnot. Great dragonflies. Horseflies as big as swallows, with huge, stinging tails. They'd sting you and bite you and gorge on your flesh and lay their eggs inside you. They'd keep giving you food and water, the Persians, pouring on that honey. They didn't want you dying of dehydration or starvation. They wanted to watch that cloud of insects grow and grow around you: bigger than a car, big as a bus, a whale. Engulfing you as you screamed all day and all night. Screaming as maggots and larvae burst out of your flesh in great clumps, your face a huge, swollen mass of boils, bites and sores. Do you know there are recorded cases of people enduring this for seventeen days before they died of sceptic shock? *Seventeen days.*' She sighed. 'Sadly, we don't have that amount of time. So I've come up with a kind of condensed version for young Walt here.'

She moved towards her bag. Please God, no.

'I think the thing that abhors us most as humans, as top-of-the-chain predators, is the idea of something feeding on us. Burrowing within us.'

She reached into the bag with both hands and hefted out a big glass Mason jar with a metal lid, the kind you see in old-fashioned sweet shops. There were airholes in the lid.

Inside the jar – a fat, black rat.

It was huge, almost completely filling the jar, with a long, wet-looking pink tail coiled around it. She set it down on the edge of the table. The rat was throwing itself at the glass, enraged, confused, its yellow teeth bared horribly. Walt started screaming into his gag, shaking his head from side to side.

'I've been starving him for weeks.'

I felt my mind coming loose. Sanity slipping away.

'Tell me, William.' She came over and knelt beside me, taking my gag out.

'Please,' I said.

'What really happened that day? What don't I know? What are you leaving out? I've had nearly

thirty years of guessing. If you're honest with me,
if I believe you, I might be persuaded to put him
back in the bag and give Walt a reasonably quick
death.'

There was no sound from Walt. He'd fainted.

'I told you.' I was crying. 'It was Banny. He –'

'Are you sure?'

'Please . . .'

It was time to go back. Back to the riverbank.

40

DOCHERTY WENT for Banny.

Instantly, you could tell he'd never been in a fight in his life: head down, fists flailing wildly. Banny, on the other hand, had been fighting since his first day at primary school; an eight-year veteran of playground battles and street fights. He stepped back and let Docherty reach him, taking a couple of weak, useless punches on the arms before he grabbed his hair and started slowly pulling Docherty's head towards the ground. 'Iya! Iya!' Docherty squealed. Banny kicked Docherty hard in the face, one, two, three times. He let him go and Docherty staggered back and fell down, blood pouring from his nose and mouth, but trying to get back up, trying to stand on trembling legs.

'C'MON THEN!' Banny screamed.

It became like a dream, like a nightmare, like a

video, like one of the horror videos watched on those endless afternoons off school, the curtains closed in the living room of the small council house, the only light coming from the fizzing television. Things happened quickly, fast-forward, and yet seemed to take all the time in the world. Freeze-frame. Slow motion. Banny lashing Docherty with the rod, shouting things I couldn't hear. Tommy, his jaw set terribly as his foot lashed back and forth, real blood on the ox-blood Doc Martens. Above us the sky was cloudless, smiling on the crime, the riverbank empty for miles in both directions. The bushes and the poured-concrete weir house bearing silent witness. Docherty's trousers were pulled off, then his pants, his trembling, bloodied hand as he tried to stop this, tried to hold onto this last shred of dignity ('no, no, no, please, no . . .'), and then the bronze rod was arcing against the blue again, the sun kissing the length of the graphite as it whistled through the air, a filament of silver line trailing behind it. The red welts appearing on his thighs, his buttocks, the blood. More blood. His face – the face I still see every night as I reach for sleep – caked in dirt and tears, a pebble stuck to his cheek, looking at me, begging. Tommy sitting on his back, Banny on his legs, moving the broken end of the rod towards . . .

His scream.

This had all gone far enough, too far, much, much too far. But there was further to go, distance yet to run, as Tommy jumped on his head now, laughing, stumbling, falling over. Then I was climbing up on the wall above Docherty and Banny was shouting 'Go oan, Wullie! Dae it!' and I was leaping off.

Me, caught against the sun.

My black silhouette framed, arms extended, feet coming down, like at the pool ('No Dive-Bombing'), like an awful bird of prey, falling, falling, my feet the talons, coming straight down at Docherty's skull, Docherty sobbing, trying to crawl, the glittering rod quivering in time with his sobs. My face, lit with terrible glee. The impact . . .

Me getting up and walking away, straightening my Harrington, brushing chalky dust off, flicking my hair out of my face.

Back into real time and the silence, broken by a gull, crying as it streaked low over the river, white on grey, moving fast in the corner of my eye. Tommy was the first to speak.

'Docherty? Get up, ya cunt.'

They'd told us something, in Physics, about the velocity of falling objects, something to with mass times gravity or something, about unstoppable forces and immovable objects, but the only person here who would have been listening, who could have told you what the equation was, wasn't listening any more. He wouldn't be listening to anything ever again.

A single rivulet from his ear – black and thick as treacle. His mouth and eyes – both open, the mouth caught as though it was forming the end of the word 'no', the eyes just staring up, staring dumbstruck at the bland, vacant sky.

I took charge.

I was smarter than them.

Nobody saw anything.

It was our word against any cunt's.

No, *don't* get stones and boulders and put them in his pockets. It'll look deliberate. We rolled him to the edge of the weir and pushed him into the water. It'll look like he fell down the bank and hit his head on the weir. The current'll probably take him all the way out to sea. He floated away, face down, just below the surface, the green parka ballooning up out of the water slightly.

I was a wee boy who did a very bad thing.

In court. The three of us sullen and bored in the dock. I did better with the child psychologists than Banny or 'feeble-minded' Tommy. We were all as bad as each other, but Banny was clearly the ringleader. His reputation at school. The testimony of teachers and social workers. Banny tried to blame me – Aye, he'd battered him, but I'd jumped on his head. I'd jumped on his head. We were all liars and manipulators, they said. We blamed each other. The real story never emerged. Banny did it. Tommy did it. I did it. Who's to say? Cannae remember. Naw. Honest, man. Dinnae ken. His fault. No mine. Didnae mean it, so we didnae.

And in the tent that time. Yes. Pushing back against him. Rubbing, letting it all happen until you juddered and saw stars and felt wetness spreading down there in the sleeping bag and Banny was wiping his hand on your back and then –

Gets all mangled in your mind over the years.

I swear I could see Banny silhouetted against the sky, jumping down, leather-soled weejuns coming down onto Docherty's skull. Cannae remember. Honest. Banny did it. Banny –

I did it.

41

SHE'D LISTENED, not saying anything, not inter-rupting the words I had never spoken to anyone. The only sound in the room now was the rat, clawing and scratching softly on glass. Walt lay unconscious on the pool table, looking strangely peaceful.

After a long time she said, 'Thank you for your honesty.'

'Please.' I was sobbing. 'Let him go. Kill me.'

I'd only ever been trespassing in happiness, my right, the very possibility, forfeited three decades ago, on that riverbank. This, or something like it, something like Banny or Tommy, pacing in a cell or bleeding to death in the showers, this was what should have happened.

She walked over to the table, picked up the jar and turned it over. A metallic thunk as the rat landed on the lid. Its tail dangled through one of the air holes, over half a foot long. Its claws grated on the metal. I started screaming. She picked up the scalpel. The rat was hurling itself at the glass, emitting a terrible screech, hopping up and down, scraping at the metal lid, its black claws scraping out of the air holes. She twisted the lid, beginning to unscrew it, the rat turning with it, oddly, madly comic. Walt began to stir, sensing something even through sleep perhaps.

I dug my teeth into the back of my tongue, feeling blood coming into my mouth. Could I do it? Bite off my tongue at the root, suck in a deep breath and drown blissfully in a fountain of my own blood? I could hear a regular thumping sound somewhere in my head and I wondered if this was what happened when you went insane.

Then the walls started to shake and she stopped.

She heard the thumping noise too.

My heart stopped as I recognised the sound, hearing it for the second time that night.

Helicopter rotors.

She ran to the windows. The six windows in the basement rec room ran all the way along the wall at head height, ground level outside. They were rectangular slits really, too small for a man to get through. The sound seemed to disappear for a moment and then it came again, much louder, and from where I lay twisted on the floor I saw a white beam of light split the night sky and begin probing the ground.

She smacked the jar back down onto the table and picked up the revolver, checking the chamber. She looked at Walt, seeming to debate something in her head, her one visible eye flipping from him to the windows, the rotors growing deafening, the helicopter seeming to be right above the house. Would she just shoot him?

'Look,' I said, frantic, speaking fast, 'it must be the police. Because they didn't check in or something. Stop all this, I . . . I won't –'

She stepped forward and kicked me hard in the face. I felt blood spurt out of my nose, coloured lights sparkling in front of my eyes as she ran out of the room.

'Walt, Walt . . .' He was weeping, yelling into the gag, his nostrils flaring as he strained at the ropes, trying to move, to pull away from the rat, just inches from his ankles, pawing, scratching, almost toppling the jar over.

'It's the police. It must be. She –'

Suddenly the helicopter came down into view through the windows, maybe thirty feet off the ground, trying to land hesitantly, as though it were a living creature, unsure of the depth of the snow. It was being buffeted from side to side in the wind, the snow below so deep it looked impossible to land. The side door on the helicopter slid open and a rope ladder dropped down, catching in the beam of light, swinging back and forth, dangling maybe ten feet above the ground. Walt and I watched as a figure started climbing down. He hung at the end of the ladder for a moment and then dropped down into the snow. Another man, then a third, did the same. As soon as they were down and clear the helicopter rose back up into black sky and – almost immediately – there was a burst of gunfire, very close to the house, and we could hear men shouting out there, the single reports of pistols, another ragged burst of automatic fire, a firefight breaking out. Something raked along the wall of the basement and two of the windows exploded inwards, showering Walt and me with glass, cold air rushing in.

42

THE SHOOTING stopped. Walt's sobbing – soft but constant. Then I heard voices outside, close to the broken windows, hushed, whispering. As I opened my mouth to scream, to tell them where we were, a deafening barrage of automatic gunfire exploded close by, rounds hitting wood and concrete along the exterior wall, a scream, the sound of feet running through the snow then silence again.

Minutes passed. Me hog-tied on the floor, Walt lashed to the pool table. I tried to move and felt stunning, dizzying pain shooting through my left leg, felt fresh, warm blood seeping from the wound in my thigh, soaking my trousers.

I heard a metallic sound.

The doorknob was turning.

I looked up, breathing hard, my eyes bulging,

and saw Old Sam in the doorway, a pistol in one hand. His jaw dropping as he saw us.

'Jesus Christ,' he whispered.

(Later, much later, I would find out about the private Gulfstream G650 he'd managed to charter from a film producer on Maui. The new Gulfstream, the only one on the island, with an operating range of 7,000 nautical miles, capable of getting all the way from the middle of the Pacific to Canada without refuelling in just over eight hours. The helicopter pilot who was paid a staggering sum to bring them out here through the storm. The incredible mountains that can be levelled when money is irrelevant.)

'Sam,' I said as he ran to the pool table, picking up the knife that lay on the edge and starting to cut Walt's bonds. He tugged the gag out and Walt collapsed into his arms crying, saying, 'Papa, Papa,' over and over. 'It's OK, boy,' Old Sam said. 'I'm here.' He started to untie me, freeing my arms first. Walt clung around his grandfather's waist, shaking, sobbing, burying his face in Old Sam's side. My legs came free and I stretched them, crying out in pain as I did so. 'Easy,' Old Sam said. 'Mike's here. He's outside.' He leaned over me, with Walt somewhere between the two of us.

'Is she dead?' I asked.

'She?' he said, his brow creasing in the half-light. Jesus.

A shape behind him, a shadow moving. Before I could scream an arm appeared, clamping round his forehead. He went to reach for the gun but too late, another arm came out – she loomed up over him now, a terrible grimace of determination on her face – and drew the scalpel quickly across his throat. I held Walt tightly into my chest, his face buried in me, as his grandfather's blood sprayed over us. It seemed to go on for a long time, her holding him tightly from behind, Old Sam juddering and kicking as he bled out, his expression one of astonishment until his eyeballs started flipping up in their sockets. Me screaming, Walt crying into me. Finally she let him fall to the floor. She dropped the scalpel and pulled the revolver from her waistband. She pressed the barrel into the small of Walt's back as he lay wriggling and crying on top of me.

'No more time, William,' she said with a sad smile.

BANGBANGBANG. Three shots rang out in quick succession and she was staggering backwards, gasping, clutching her chest, dropping the gun and stumbling over in the doorway, two more shots smashing into the door frame, blowing off chunks of wood as she fell into the hallway and vanished. I turned to see a man's arms protruding through one of the broken slit windows, a revolver clamped marksman-style between his fists. 'MIKE!' I screamed.

'Stay there, Donnie. I can't get through here. I'm coming through the house to get you. OK?'

'NO! She's —'

'Donnie, I just put three .38 shells in her chest. She's down, OK?'

He disappeared. I cradled Walt, who had his hands pressed against his ears, and sat up.

'Where's Grandapa?' Walt asked.

'He'll be OK,' I said. I had Walt's face pressed tight into my neck now, holding him away from his grandfather's corpse, the huge bloodstain spreading out from under his face. 'Don't look.' I growled with pain as I got to my feet, holding onto the arm of a chair, pushing us up using only my right leg, pain sparkling through the left one. Stumbling forward in the semi-darkness I edged towards the doorway.

No body in the hall. She was gone.

I glanced up and down the long, dark hallway. Nothing.

Officer Hudson's black bra — the blood pooling on her bare skin.

KNOCK KNOCK.

Fear reigniting.

The doorway I was standing in was the only way out of the rec room and into the rest of the house. I hobbled back to the window, holding Walt. The bottom of the slit was level with my chin, tiny shards of ragged glass sticking up from it, like teeth. About a hundred yards away sat the police helicopter. In the distance, somewhere above the horizon, I could see lightness amid the black and grey night, the first streaks of dawn.

'Listen, Walt, listen to me,' I whispered. 'You can get through this window. I can't. I want you to run out to the police helicopter, get in the back, and lock yourself in. OK?'

'NO!'

'Shhh, Walt. Please. Listen. Mike's here. You know Uncle Mike? He'll stop her. But I need you to go and hide just now, OK?

'*DONNIE? WALT?*' Mike Rawls's voice came from somewhere deep in the house behind us.

'See?' I said. 'Now please, Walt. Quickly. Watch the glass.' I pushed him up to the slit and he scrambled through and took off running.

'*DONNIE?*' Mike's voice closer now, somewhere down the hall.

I watched until Walt reached the chopper, opened

the rear door, and climbed in. I picked up Old Sam's pistol and popped the magazine; fat brass cartridges nestling all the way up to the top. I slid it back home and limped to the doorway. I crouched down, looking down the hall, towards the living area, in the direction of Mike's voice. It was pitch black in the interior of the house, you couldn't see more than a couple of feet in front of you.

'Mike! Be careful. She's not hurt. She's got a bulletproof vest on.'

'Help's on its way.' His voice came disembodied down the long hallway. 'Are you armed?'

'Yes.'

'Then stay put. They'll be here in a few minutes. Lady.' He raised his voice, shouting to the empty house. 'This is over. Come on out and give yourself up.'

Silence. Darkness. I pressed myself against the wall, the gun held tightly in front of me. Directly across the corridor from me lay the open door to one of the guest bedrooms. It connected to a bathroom, then onto another bedroom on the other side. Suddenly, in the periphery of my vision, I thought I saw a change in the density of the blackness through the doorway, something moving fast across the bedroom. I screamed and fired three times, the muzzle flash briefly lighting up the hallway, strobing madly as I blew holes in the drywall, the concussion ringing in my ears.

'It's her! Mike! She's moving towards you! Mike!'

'Stay where you are, Donnie!'

I strained to listen, my ears ringing but my eyes gradually adjusting to the darkness. To my right the long hallway stretched off towards four steps that led up into the living area, towards Mike's voice. To my left lay the utility room, with its connecting door to the big garage.

Moments passed in silence.

I heard a noise far away, up towards Mike, something breaking, or falling over, then Mike was shouting 'HOLD IT!' then two sharp reports, a fast *BANGBANG* and the sound of something heavy hitting the floor, then silence. I hugged the wall, trembling, the gun pointed straight ahead of me.

'Donnie?' Relief as Mike's voice came back down the hallway. 'Stay put. I'm going to check on the body.'

I could hear him in the distance, boards creaking as he moved across the hardwood floor, moving further away from me. I crawled forward on my elbows, the fear anesthetising the pain in my leg now, poking my head out into the corridor, the gun extended in front of me. Silence. Then something very faint, like a grunt or a gasp.

'MIKE! MIKE!' I shouted into the darkness.

I became aware of a wet, pattering sound from somewhere far down the hallway, like water from a burst pipe spattering onto wood. Maybe the shooting had damaged a —

The house lights erupted back on, blinding me.

I looked up and saw her move out of the shadows and reveal herself at the top of the short flight of stairs, maybe seventy feet away.

She looked like she'd been dipped in blood.

I started screaming.

Her arms were extended, the butcher's knife in one hand, the chrome revolver in the other, showing them to me.

I kept screaming as I brought the pistol up and started firing, seeing her disappear in the muzzle flash, ducking left as I blew holes all around where she had been, hitting the walls and the ceiling, turning the gun left and pumping the trigger, blowing holes in the drywall she disappeared behind, my ears singing, thick cordite smoke choking me as I kept pumping the trigger and screaming and then the slide locked open, the gun scalding hot in my hands and the trigger clacking uselessly, and I was throwing the empty gun down and running, careering down the hallway away from her, blood sloshing in my left trainer.

43

I BURST into the utility room and stood panting, clutching my leg amid the washer, the dryer and the plastic wicker baskets. The clothes horse, the bottles of detergent and fabric softener and the laundry smell; the ultra totems of domesticity madly, incongruently alien. I could hear her coming thumping down the hallway and I froze – weaponless, defenceless.

Through the door and into the garage, feeling the drop in temperature as I came into the huge, fluorescent-lit, breeze-block space we used as extra storage. I pulled the flimsy deadbolt on the door behind me and looked around. Up at the far end was an assortment of packing crates, boxes and old furniture. A workbench with some tools. An axe for splitting wood.

I grabbed the axe and bolted for the back of the

garage just as I heard the door into the laundry room being kicked open behind me. Threading my way through the crates and boxes, I crouched down and tried not to breathe. The door was rattling, then banging as she started kicking it. Five or six hard kicks before the wood splintered, the door flew open and she came down the steps.

I was only thirty or forty feet away and it took all my strength not to scream out loud at the sight of her brightly lit under the cold strip lighting. The blood. She was *soaked* in blood. She looked around the garage and started scraping the knife along the barrel of the gun, like she was sharpening it. I cradled the axe as she came nearer. Twenty feet away.

'*William . . . William.*' Her voice in sing-song was terrible. Ten feet. So close. 'I might just go and find Walt and get it over with. I think you must have sent him out to hide in that helicopter . . .' She turned away from me.

I leapt out, the axe cocked back and already coming down towards her. She wheeled, gun extended, the shaft of the axe smashing into her arm, the gun going down and off, the shot deafening off the breeze-block walls.

Searing heat.

The blast from the Python disintegrating my left

thigh, firing straight into the knife wound, obliterating tissue and bone, sending me screaming onto the oil-stained floor. Faint now, on the verge of passing out as she climbed on top of me, her face just inches from mine, blood (hers? Mike's?) dripping onto my face. I could feel her working with the knife, slicing at me, cutting something off.

Finished now.

She came up with a long strip of my shirt and started tying it around my leg, above the gunshot wound, tugging it tightly. 'You need to live, William. Live.'

Oh, Sam. Oh, Walt. I'm sorry. I could see their faces swimming in front of me now.

'There.' She was sitting on my chest. 'I'm going to go and kill Walt now, William. I'll just stab him to death, I think. I'll leave the face so you can view the body. Then I'll put the gun in my mouth and I'll be gone.'

The gun. It was lying on the floor, next to her knee, just inches from my right hand. I punched it and sent it skittering away a few feet. She brought the knife up and held it in front of my face. 'Don't be silly.' I brought my left hand up, palm outwards and open, almost like I was going to high-five her, and brought it down straight onto the point of the knife, forcing it down hard, the eight-inch blade skewering my palm as I pushed down, the cut widening – two inches, three – as the blade passed out the back of my hand. I felt no pain. She looked confused, puzzled, as I clamped my good right leg around her waist, holding her tightly. I grabbed her knife wrist with my right hand and started twisting the blade towards her. She began tugging, trying to pull the knife out, to free it, but I kept going, pulling her down towards me with the right leg, pushing the knife towards her with both hands, the cold metal skewering my left palm grating, feeling terrible and alien, my blood streaming down the chequered metal grip. She slashed at my face with her free hand, tearing my cheek open with her nails. She went to do it again and I snapped up at her and got her thumb between my teeth, biting down savagely, hearing her scream, tasting coppery blood spurting into my mouth, the two of us locked in an insane death grip now, like wrestlers in an intricate knot, sweat pouring down my face, and still I kept pushing up with the knife, pulling her forward with my good leg, feeling the muscles in that leg begin to rend and tear, unable even to feel my left leg any more as she tried to rip her thumb out of my mouth, feeling my teeth grinding against bone, the point of the knife just inches from her throat now. In desperation she suddenly let go of the handle of the knife and lunged for the gun. I grabbed the back of her head with my right hand and pulled her down towards me, fixing the handle of the knife against my chest so hard it felt like my breastbone might crack, my left hand still skewered upon it, the blade pointing straight up as I brought her down onto it. With everything I had, everything I was, I forced her chin onto the tip of the blade, the knife entering the soft flesh at the bottom of her chin, beneath her mouth. Using my right hand on the back of her head, rising up off the floor with the effort, I pulled her skull towards me and heard a soft crack. I could see the blade moving up through her mouth, through her tongue, skewering her tongue to the roof of her mouth.

'Mmmff. Urrr,' she said.

A louder crack, like you hear when boning a chicken, as the knife broke through the bone in the roof of her mouth. Blood pouring out of her mouth, all over me, as I pulled harder and felt something give, saw a ridge actually appearing under the flesh beside her nose as the blade passed upwards, deep into her skull, somewhere behind her eyes now, her eyes flickering as though she were trying to see what was happening in there.

Her eyes locked dreadfully onto mine, burning with thirty years of hatred. I pulled as hard as I could and the knife slid all the way up, her chin smacking down onto the back of my impaled hand while, with my right hand stretched over the top of her head, I actually felt the tip of the blade knock against the inside of her skull. With a sigh she shuddered and went limp, a deadweight, the kebab formed by the butt of the knife, then my hand, then her head.

I fell back, drenched with sweat and gore.

Suddenly I was aware of how wet the floor beneath me was. I had broken the crude tourniquet during the struggle and blood was flowing from what remained of my left leg. We lay there in this strange embrace. I stared at the strip lighting above me, the glow from the tubes seeming to spread out, to envelop the whole room in a white fizz.

'I'm sorry,' I mumbled.

To her? To Sammy? To Walt? To all the people she'd killed because of what I'd done? I didn't know. The white fizz was increasing, surrounding me like warm snow, the snow that surrounded the house, that enveloped this part of the world so much. And then I saw Sammy and Walt in the snow, running after Herby, laughing and throwing snowballs. I'm somewhere behind them, off in the distance, to one side, half in shadow, where I spent much of my life. The sun is warm above us, reflecting off the snow, creating a steadily brightening glare, the glare growing in intensity, blotting everything out, everything except a steady, rhythmical thumping noise, Sammy and Walt looking up into the sky now, shielding their eyes, trying to see something I cannot see. Because the glare is drowning everything now, Sammy and Walt and Herby and the landscape disappearing, fading like a photograph dropped in water, everything becoming white, and I am leaving my body and becoming part of it and I am glad to go.

I'm sorry.

Goodbye.

Walt.

Postscript

Coldwater, Florida

FIFTEEN PINTS. Nearly two gallons. I sometimes think of it that way when I'm gassing up the car; after my finger's been on the trigger for however long it takes to pump two gallons, I'll think, 'That's how much they gave me.' Or four quarts. That'll cross my mind at the supermarket, buying milk. I'll picture four of those big quart milk jugs, brimming with blood.

They did what they could with my leg, but there was so much tissue loss. It aches most of the time, but I get along well enough with the painkillers and the cane.

It hasn't been as easy to fix Walt. He cries for his mother a lot, at night, when he wakes from the dreams he has to endure. He adjusted to having nine fingers better than he adjusted to losing the

316

less tangible things she removed. He was prescribed strong sedatives for a time, but they left him stumbling and sluggish all day. We gradually weaned him off them, but now I lie awake most nights listening for the screams that will send me running to his bedroom. 'She's coming!' He'll be crying and I'll slip my arms around him and whisper, 'It's OK, you're safe. I'm here. Daddy's here.' Sometimes I'll catch him looking at me and I wonder if he's thinking about the things I did, the things he heard that night. We don't discuss it together, only in therapy.

Neither of us went to the funeral. Sammy and her father, buried on the same day, in the family plot outside Regina. It was huge news. I was still in the ICU and Walt was pretty much catatonic. Months later he asked to see his mom's grave and I took him up there. He didn't cry, couldn't seem to make the connection that the bones of the woman who loved him and nurtured him were laid under his feet. I tried not to think about what was under there. That video. The morgue. She killed nine people, Gill Docherty, aka Irene Kramer. I list their names here.

Paul Cardew
Samantha Myers

Sgt Richard Danko, Regina PD
Officer Sara Hudson, Regina PD
Sgt Matt Helm, Regina PD
Jan Franklin
William Robertson
Samuel Myers
Michael Rawls

Collectively these people left behind more than sixty close relatives; partners, parents, children. Who can count the sleepless nights, the screaming and crying? The empty hours spent staring into space, imagining their ends, their final moments. Because murder is a cluster bomb, a daisy-cutter, napalm, levelling all around it, spreading pain and destruction down the years, far beyond its epicentre.

We have a lot of money, Walt and I (Sammy's estate, the insurance), and, in theory, when his grandmother dies, we will get a lot more. But there is litigation in process, Mrs Myers claiming my marriage to her daughter was fraudulent, illegal. She is angry and doubly bereaved. She wants to make sure that Walt inherits everything when he is twenty-one. That it does not come to me as his guardian if she dies before that. I don't care. I won't fight it.

With the money, without a job and the lack of friends or family, comes time to think. What happened that day on the riverbank, in those frenzied moments that would entrain the loss and ruin of so many lives? 'As flies to wanton boys . . .' Mr Cardew said. But I was worse than that, worse than Tommy, worse than Banny the bully. I was the bully's lackey, his acolyte, knowing that terrible wrong was being done but looking to impress anyway, to impress by outdoing. 'If everybody else jumped off a bridge, would you?' they used to say, back in my time and place. Yes. A bigger bridge. A higher bridge. That low stone wall, me leaping high in the air, caught against the spring sunshine, caught in the gleeful, astonished gazes of my friends.

Reading, always reading here in the Florida sunshine, I came across a definition of hell somewhere – maybe in Joyce? – which said that the sinner is forced to spend his time in hell in the company of the people with whom he committed his worst sins. Often, when I try to think of Sammy, when I try to reach for a comforting image of her to ease me into sleep – her voice, her face, a moment we shared – it is her near namesake I find waiting for me in the recesses of my mind, with his swagger, his words, his spittle hitting the ground as he straightens his Harrington. Yes. It is right, it is salutary, that I should spend so much time in Banny's company.

Walt is nearly eleven now. Almost the same age as Craig was when we killed him. (*You see? You still can't say it. When we killed him? When you killed him.*) No one at school knows how he lost his pinkie, what really happened to him. My son has a back-story too now. My legacy to him. (*'And he punishes the children for the sins of the fathers . . .'*)

Sometimes, when I watch Walt lost in a rare moment of play, or made childishly happy by an unexpected treat or favour, the way the face flowers so brightly, opening out towards you, I understand her best. I picture the boy fished from a river after days and laid broken and sightless on a metal slab and her rage floods me like wine, heady and intox-icating, making me sway on the balls of my feet. Every parent has easy mental access to this wind tunnel. You think about your response – about the knife, the gun, the baseball bat. How many are afforded the opportunity to step into it in the real world? I have come across a few examples here on the sofa, or out by the palm-fringed pool, lightly smeared with Valium, a strong drink by my side and a warm book in my lap. The German father of boys murdered and daughters raped by Russian troops, Russian troops who were very soon outflanked and captured themselves. The *Wehrmacht* officer allowed him his time in the barn with two of the guilty men. He ignored the proffered Walther and went to work with shears and a chair leg. And against that – the Muslim father praying for clemency for the drunks who mowed down his son in a stolen car. The responses to atrocity as varied as human belief itself.

Or this, from an essay by George Orwell. I wrote the quotation out in one of the yellow legal pads I keep on my desk in the study.

> Properly speaking, there is no such thing as revenge. Revenge is an act which you want to commit when you are powerless and because you are powerless: as soon as the sense of impotence is removed, the desire evaporates also.

Orwell wrote this in Allied Occupied Europe in 1945, after witnessing the cruelties perpetrated on captured Nazi soldiers. And, despite my own experience, I think Orwell is, on the whole, right. Most people, given the chance to abuse or torment someone who had once done the same to them, would turn away. In most of us the half-life of hatred is short.

But not in everyone.

Some people can keep it alive in the breast for many years. And even then most of these people, if they were offered the opportunity to avenge their wrong, to pluck the eyeball or the tooth that they are due, most of them would still turn and walk away.

But not all of them. A few will reach into their bag and start taking things out. They'll pour the ether onto the gauze and walk straight towards you. They'll scrape the knife along the gun barrel as they come looking for you in the dark. And when you call out for help, for your mother or for your God, they will not hear you. They'll smile and keep on coming.

I remember the day over twenty years ago that Mr Cardew gave me the *Complete Shakespeare*, the day I got the three Highers (ABB) that satisfied my conditional offer from Lampeter. I had been Donnie for over a year then and neither of us slipped very often. William was gone. We'd talked of practical things, about what I could expect at university, about the halfway house I'd live in for a few months over the remainder of the summer, to acclimatise before term began and I took up a place in the halls of residence. He'd be visiting me. 'Don't go getting drunk out of your mind at any of these freshers' parties now,' he'd said, smiling, as he extended his hand. We shook, there in that sad room where so much had happened in the last seven years, where Wilfred Owen's rifles had stuttered, where Birnham Wood had walked to Dunsinane, where Ted Hughes's Jaguar had prowled. He left the book on the table and I read the inscription after he'd gone. *Now make yourself proud.*

But I couldn't, not without telling the truth. The truth he never knew. Without saying 'I did it. It was me.' I've only ever said it aloud to one person, but she was the person who'd needed to hear it the most. A kind of peace, then.

Down the hall I can hear Cora clattering pots in the kitchen. I can smell an aromatic stew. Soon enough it will be six o'clock and I can fix myself a drink. (In the immediate aftermath I found myself drinking during the day. I pushed it back, slowly, gradually, to 6 p.m. I smiled with recognition when I read an interview with J. G. Ballard, who said he started drinking all day to cope in the aftermath of his wife's death, to cope with raising several children on his own. Ballard too finally pushed it back to a six o'clock start. 'Was that hard?' the interviewer asked him. 'Hard?' Ballard said. 'It was like Stalingrad.')

I look up from my book as, through the open

windows, I hear the squawk of brakes, then the hiss of hydraulics and the flap-bang of the concertina doors opening, then the chatter of children. I get up from my desk, wincing, using my hands to push myself up, and head through the cool, airy house to greet my son.

JOHN NIVEN

Kill Your Friends

Meet Steven Stelfox.

It's London 1997: New Labour is sweeping into power and Britpop is at its zenith. A&R man Stelfox is slashing and burning his way through the music industry, fuelled by greed and inhuman quantities of cocaine, searching for the next hit record amid a relentless orgy of self-gratification.

But as the hits dry up and the industry begins to change, Stelfox must take the notion of cut-throat business practices to murderous new levels in a desperate attempt to salvage his career.

'Magnificently eloquent ... A vicious black-hearted howl of a book ... cripplingly funny'
THE TIMES

'The filthiest, blackest, most shocking, most hilarious debut novel I've read in years'
INDIA KNIGHT

'Might well be the best British novel since Trainspotting'
WORD

'Wonderfully nasty ... Extraordinarily vicious, deeply cynical and thoroughly depraved, but it's also bed-wettingly funny'
SCOTSMAN

JOHN NIVEN

The Amateurs

GARY is a sweet and decent man. Only two things would improve his life – having children with his gorgeous wife Pauline, and a lower golf handicap. Both are unlikely.

PAULINE is wondering how she ended up living in an ugly little house, driving a second-hand car and making a living dressing up as Tinkerbell. She is planning to leave Gary for a self-made carpet millionaire.

FINDLAY, the Carpet King of Scotland, wants to trade in his obese wife for a younger model. But if he goes for a divorce she'll take him to the cleaners. If only there was some way she could be made to disappear …

LEE, Gary's luckless brother, has botched one too many drug deals. Local crime overlord Ranta Campbell gives him one more job – one last chance to get it right. Lee's done some bad things – but murder?

When Gary gets smashed on the head by a golf ball and miraculously develops an absolutely perfect swing, everyone finds their fates rest on the final day of the Open Championship.

'Gripping, sexy, violent and outrageous'
MIRROR

'Screamingly funny'
SCOTSMAN

JOHN NIVEN

The Second Coming

SENT FROM HEAVEN ... RAISING HELL

God takes a look at the Earth around the time of the Renaissance and everything looks pretty good – so he takes a holiday. In Heaven-time this is just a week's fishing trip, but on Earth several hundred years go by. When God returns, he finds all hell has broken loose: world wars, holocausts, famine, capitalism and 'fucking Christians everywhere'. There's only one thing for it. They're sending the kid back.

JC, reborn, is a struggling musician in New York City, trying to teach the one true commandment: Be Nice! His best chance to win hearts and minds is to enter *American Pop Star*. But the number one show in America is the unholy creation of a record executive who's more than a match for the Son of God ... Steven Stelfox.

'*Confrontational, blasphemous ... and bloody funny*'
INDEPENDENT ON SUNDAY

'*Believe me, this book is going to cause one almighty stink ... Niven provides hilarious, perceptive entertainment ... Only the truly ignorant will take offence. But then they usually do*'
HENRY SUTTON, DAILY MIRROR

'*Jesus battles oppression, hypocrisy and the satanic forces of Simon Cowell – sorry, "Steven Stelfox" ... funny and smart*'
INDEPENDENT

John Niven

Straight White Male

Kennedy Marr, a novelist from the old school and borderline alcoholic, is writing film scripts in LA, insulting his way through Californian society, and trying to screw every woman he meets. But he's also suffering from writer's block and unpaid taxes. Then a solution presents itself – Marr is to be the unlikely recipient of a prize for outstanding contribution to modern literature, an award worth half a million pounds. The catch? He must spend a year teaching at the English university where his ex-wife and estranged daughter now reside.

As Kennedy acclimatises to the sleepy campus, he's forced to reconsider his precarious lifestyle. Incredible as it may seem, there might actually be a father and a teacher lurking inside this 'preening, narcissistic, priapic sociopath'. Or is there…?

'I cried three times and laughed fifty. Magnificent.'
CAITLIN MORAN

'Straight White Male is a heartbreaker; a poignant literary treatise on the all-too-moral battle between human individual desire and social need.'
IRVINE WELSH

'Funny as hell and moving.'
IAN RANKIN

'Addictive … hilarious.'
DANNY WALLACE